BORN
SCARED

BORN
SCARED

KEVIN BROOKS

CANDLEWICK PRESS

Copyright © 2016 by Kevin Brooks

Lines on pp. 129–130 from *Martyn Pig* by Kevin Brooks (© Kevin Brooks, 2002) reproduced courtesy of Chicken House.
Lyric on p. 164 from "Merry Xmas Everybody" (© Holder/Lea, 1973) reproduced courtesy of Barn Publishing (Slade) Limited.

First U.S. edition 2018

First published by Electric Monkey, an imprint of Egmont U.K. Limited 2016

Library of Congress Catalog Card Number pending
ISBN 978-0-7636-9565-1

18 19 20 21 22 23 LSC 10 9 8 7 6 5 4 3 2 1

Printed in Crawfordsville, IN, U.S.A.

This book was typeset in Perpetua.

Candlewick Press
99 Dover Street
Somerville, Massachusetts 02144

visit us at www.candlewick.com

BORN
SCARED

1

CHRISTMAS EVE

I'm as far as the hallway now. Coat, hat, boots, gloves . . .

Cold sweat running down my back.

It's three o'clock in the afternoon, Christmas Eve.

The snowstorm's getting worse.

My heart's pounding. I'm shaking, shivering. I feel sick. And every cell in my body is screaming at me to turn around and run.

But I can't move.

Either way.

I can't go back.

Can't go out.

I can't do it.

It's impossible.

I can't go out there.

I'm terrified.

2

LESS THAN NOTHING

My fear pills are yellow, which isn't a bad color for me.

Red is blood (and Santas), black is death, blue is the drowning sea . . .

Yellow is cheese and bananas.

And pills.

I don't know why I call them fear pills. They're antifear pills really.

I'm chronically afraid of almost everything.

Sometimes I think I can remember being scared when I was still in my mother's womb. It's not much more than a distant feeling really, and I have no idea what I could have been frightened of in there, or how — in my unformed state — I could have perceived it.

Unless . . .

Unless.

It's probably more accurate to say that I sometimes think I can remember being scared when *we* were still in *our* mother's womb. There were two of us in there: me and my sister, Ellamay. We were twins, and I know in my heart that my embryonic fears — if that's what they were — were as much Ellamay's as they were mine.

We were scared.

Together.

We were as one.

As we still are now.

And perhaps we knew what was coming. Perhaps we were frightened because we knew one of us was dying . . .

No, I don't think that's it.

I don't think any of us knows what death is until it's explained to us. And the strange thing about that is that although there must be a pivotal moment in all our lives when we find out for the first time that all living things die, and that at some point in the future our own life will come to an end, I certainly can't remember the moment when I found out, and I'd be surprised if anyone else can either.

Which is kind of weird, don't you think?

What I *can* remember though is the effect that moment had on me.

I don't know how old I was at the time — four? five? six? —

but I clearly remember lying in bed at night with my head beneath the covers trying to imagine death. The total absence of everything. No life, no darkness, no light. Nothing to see, nothing to feel, nothing to know. No time, no where or when, no nothing, forever and ever and ever and ever . . .

It was terrifying.

It still is.

. . . lying there for hours and hours, staring long and hard into the darkness, searching for that unimaginable emptiness, but all I ever see is a vast swathe of absolute blackness stretching deep into space for a thousand million miles, and I know that's not enough. I know that when I die there'll be no blackness and no thousand million miles, there won't even be nothing, there'll be less than nothing . . .

And the thought of that still fills my eyes with tears.

But sometimes . . .

Sometimes.

Sometimes it feels as if that memory doesn't belong to me, that it happened to someone else. Or maybe I read about it in a book or something — a story about a mixed-up kid who lies in bed at night trying to imagine death — and I identified with it so much that over time I gradually convinced myself that *I* was that mixed-up kid, and his imaginations were mine.

Not that it makes any difference, I suppose.

A memory is a memory, wherever it comes from.

I've sunk down to the hallway floor now, and I'm just sitting here with my eyes closed and my back against the wall. I'm trying to breathe steadily, trying to calm my thumping heart, trying to empty my mind.

After a while, Ellamay comes to me, her silent voice as comforting as ever.

It's all right, Elliot. It'll be okay.

"I'm scared."

I know. But you won't be alone. I'll be with you all the way.

"I don't think I can do it."

Yes, you can.

"It's too much."

You have to do it, Elliot.

"I know."

For Mum.

"I know."

For us.

We were born prematurely, at twenty-six weeks. I weighed just under a pound; Ella was even smaller. It was a traumatic birth, and at first the doctors weren't sure if any of us were going to survive. Mum had lost a lot of blood and was in a really bad way, and while she was rushed off for an emergency operation, Ellamay and I were taken to the neonatal intensive care unit, where we were put in incubators and hooked up to all kinds of stuff to keep us alive.

It didn't work for Ellamay.

She only lived for an hour.

I almost went with her.

Our hearts stopped beating at virtually the same time. But although the doctors and nurses somehow managed to save me, they couldn't do anything to bring Ella back.

Part of me died with her, and part of her lived on with me.

We're dead and alive together.

The first time I experienced fear in the outside world — as opposed to the inner world of my mother's womb — was the first time I woke up in the incubator after Ella had died. It's a moment that's as much a part of me as all the other things that make me what I am — my heart, my brain, my flesh, my blood.

I was just lying there — on my back, my eyes open — looking up through the clear-plastic dome of the incubator at the white sky of the ceiling above. Muted sounds were drifting all around me — soft beeps, hushed voices, a low humming — and although I didn't know what these noises were, I wasn't scared of them. They were the sounds of my world, as normal to me as the sound of my own stuttered breathing.

Then, all at once, everything changed.

The white sky suddenly darkened as three unknown things

appeared out of nowhere and loomed down over me. I didn't know what they were — moving things, menacing things, things that made strange jabbering noises — *wah thah . . . pah banah . . . al tah plah . . . tah yah ah lah . . .*

Monsters.

Then one of them moved even closer to me, stooping down over the incubator, getting bigger and bigger all the time . . . and that was when the fear erupted inside me. It was uncontrollable, overwhelming, absolute.

Pure terror.

It was all I was.

The three unknown things that day were my mum, her older sister Shirley, and Dr. Gibson, and the funny (peculiar) thing about it is that although they were the first people to scare me to death, they've since become the only three people who *don't* scare me to death.

They are, to me, the only true people in the world.

Everyone else is a monkem.

3

Cheap and Nasty

The two men in the stolen Land Rover were both dressed as Santa Claus. The Santa disguises had been a last-minute decision, and because it was Christmas Eve, most of the local shops and costume rental places had run out of Santa suits. The only store that hadn't sold out was the PoundCrusher at the retail park in Catterick, and the only reason they had any left was that their costumes were so cheap and nasty that Scrooge himself wouldn't have bought one. The red nylon they were made from was so thin it was virtually see-through, and the stringy white trim on the hats and jackets was glued on rather than stitched. Parts of the trim were already falling off, the loose white threads sticking to the static cling of the flimsy red nylon like dandruff. Both of the costumes were XXL—the only size left in the shop—and since neither of the two men were anywhere near "extra extra large" they'd had to make some rough-and-ready adjustments to their outfits. Extra holes had been made in the belts, sleeves and pant legs were rolled up, and the Santa hats had been made to fit by wearing beanie hats underneath. The costumes didn't include Santa boots, so both men were wearing sneakers.

4

So Many Other Things

The worst time for Mum was the first couple of years of my life when all I did was scream and cry almost constantly. People kept telling her not to worry — it's perfectly normal for babies to cry all the time — but she knew this was different. I wasn't just crying like a normal baby, I was bawling and howling, trembling all over, cowering away from just about everything.

"It's not right, is it?" Mum said to Dr. Gibson. "There's something seriously wrong with him."

The Doc looked at me — I was cradled in Mum's arms — then turned back to Mum. "I don't know what it is, Grace. I honestly don't. The only irregularities that have shown up on his regular hospital checkups are a faster-than-average heart rate and high blood pressure, but considering the trauma he went through at birth, it's perfectly understandable for him to have an instinctive fear of the hospital environment."

"But his heart rate and blood pressure go up when you're examining him too," Mum pointed out.

"Not as much as when he's at the hospital. And again, it's only natural for him to be scared of me when he knows I'm going to be prodding him and sticking needles in him."

"No," Mum said firmly, shaking her head, "there's more to it than that. I could understand it if he only got upset and agitated when he's being examined, but there are so many other things that bring it on too — unfamiliar people, strange sounds, cars, birds, dogs, rain, wind, darkness . . . he's terrified of the dark, Owen. I mean, he's not just frightened of it — I could under- stand that — he's absolutely *petrified* of it. He's never once slept without a light on."

The Doc frowned and scratched his head. "Well, physically, there doesn't seem to be anything wrong with him. As I said, the hospital checkups have all been clear, and you know yourself that I've been testing him for everything I can possibly think of — heart, liver, blood, allergies, infections — and I haven't found anything out of the ordinary." He paused, hesitating for a second, glancing at me again. "The only thing I can think of at the moment is that the underlying cause of his extreme agitation isn't directly physical."

"What do you mean?"

"The symptoms we've been talking about — increased heart rate, high blood pressure — are classic indicators of fear and anxiety, and while I still think it's fairly normal for Elliot to have an instinctive fear of the hospital, and—to a lesser extent—me, it's possible that his problems have a psychological basis rather than a specific physical cause."

Mum's face visibly paled.

"It's not uncommon, Grace," the Doc said, putting a reassuring hand on her arm. "Small babies have all kinds of curious problems, and sometimes we simply don't know what's wrong with them. And of course, they can't tell us anything themselves until they start talking. But in my experience, by the time they *do* start talking, the vast majority of them have left these problems behind."

"The vast majority?" Mum said, raising an eyebrow.

"Elliot's going to be okay, Grace," the Doc said softly. "Trust me, everything's going to be fine."

Everything wasn't fine, though. I didn't leave my problems behind. And by the time I was talking well enough to express my feelings, there was no doubt what was wrong with me.

"I'm scared, Mummy."

"Scared of what, love?"

"Everything."

5

Solid Gold Buttons

The Santa in the passenger seat of the stolen Land Rover pulled down his stringy white beard and cursed again as he scratched his unshaven chin.

"This is killing me," he said, flicking angrily at the beard. "It feels like it's made of asbestos or something."

"Put it back on," the Santa in the driver's seat told him.

"I don't see why——"

"Put it back on."

The driver's voice was calm and measured, but there was a chilling edge to it that his companion knew better than to ignore. He'd seen firsthand what his partner could do to people who didn't take him seriously, and although they *were* partners——of a kind, at least——he knew that didn't make any difference. Partner or not, if the man sitting beside him wanted to hurt him, he wouldn't think twice about doing it.

"I was only saying," he muttered, pulling the elasticated beard back up and refixing it to his face.

"Yeah, well don't, okay?"

The Santa in the passenger seat shrugged sulkily, then turned away and gazed out of the window.

It was 11:42 a.m.

They were taking the back way to the village, driving across the moors, and the Santa in the passenger seat knew this area like the back of his hand. He used to come up here with his friends when he was a kid, happily ignoring the KEEP OUT! MILITARY FIRING RANGE warning signs to search for anything the army had left behind after their maneuvers the night before — spent rifle shells, burned-out flares, even live ammunition, if you were lucky. He knew that on a clear day you could see for miles up here, all the way across to the distant Hambleton Hills, but today the snow was so thick and heavy that visibility was practically nil. The raw moorland wind was blowing so fiercely that great sheets of snow were gusting horizontally across the desolate landscape, and he could feel the car struggling to stay in a straight line.

As he rested his head against the cold glass of the window, he wondered once again what he was doing here. *Why do you keep getting yourself into these things?* he asked himself. *I mean, what's your problem? What's so difficult about saying no?*

His name was Leonard Dacre. Most people called him Dake.

The driver's name was Carl Jenner.

"When this is all over," Jenner said, breaking the silence, "you can go out and buy yourself the most expensive Santa Claus costume in the world." He glanced at Dake. "Solid gold buttons, silk pants, a snakeskin belt . . ."

"A beard made from polar bear fur . . ."

"Yeah."

The two men grinned at each other, and the Land Rover drove on through the snow.

6

BIG MONKEY TEETH

I don't like hiding things from Mum—it makes me feel like I'm betraying her—but I learned a long time ago that sometimes it's best for both of us if I keep certain things to myself.

Like Ellamay, for example.

I was about four years old when I first realized that I had to keep Ellamay to myself. The Doc had been around to see me, and afterward—while he was talking to Mum—I was sitting on the floor looking through one of my favorite picture books, and it just so happened that Ellamay suddenly came to me.

Are you all right, Elliot? she asked. *What did the Doc say this time?*

"He wants me to see a special doctor," I told her.

What kind of special doctor?

"A brain doctor."

Why?

"To stop me being frightened."

"Elliot?"

It wasn't Ellamay's voice this time, and for a second I didn't know what was happening. Then Mum spoke again.

"What are you doing, Elliot? Who are you talking to?"

I looked up at her. "It's Ellamay."

"Who?"

"Ellamay."

Mum looked puzzled, and as she turned to the Doc, I could see that she was worried too.

"Who's Ellamay, Elliot?" the Doc asked me.

"My sister."

"Your sister?"

I nodded.

The Doc turned to Mum. "Ellamay?"

Mum shook her head, and I could see now that there were tears in her eyes. "He didn't get it from me . . ." she muttered, her voice catching in her throat. "You know I couldn't bear to give her a name . . . he must have made it up himself . . ."

"Have you heard him talking to her before?"

"I always thought he was just talking to himself."

She was crying now, tears running down her face. I got up and went over to her and put my arms around her neck.

"Don't cry, Mummy. I'm sorry, I didn't mean to make you cry."

"It's all right, darling," she said, sobbing. "It's not your fault . . ."

But it *was* my fault. Who else's fault could it have been?

And ever since then, I only talk out loud to Ellamay when we're alone.

Another thing I learned not to say out loud was "monkem." Monkems are all the people in the world except for Mum, Auntie Shirley, and the Doc. They're called monkems because they come to me in my dreams as horrible scary things with hairy monkey bodies and long grasping arms and bandy legs and little human heads with vicious grinning mouths with their lips pulled back over nasty big monkey teeth . . .

That's what other people are to me.

Terrible things that want to rip me apart and eat me.

Monkems.

The first time I said it in front of Mum she told me I mustn't say it anymore.

"Why not?" I asked her.

"You can't call people monkeys, Elliot."

"Mon*kems*," I corrected her. "Not mon*keys*."

"Well, that's as may be," she said (which made no sense to me at all), "but people might *think* you're saying monkey, like I just did, and they might think you're being horrible to them."

She gave me a look. "You don't want anyone to think you're being horrible to them, do you?"

I told her I didn't, and since then I only ever use the word when I'm on my own or with Ellamay. Not that it makes any difference. The way I react to monkems — screaming my head off and running away in terror — they must think I'm crazy anyway, so what does it matter if they think I'm horrible as well? And besides, even at that age — three or four years old — I was very rarely seeing anyone else apart from Mum and Shirley and the Doc, so the chances of me upsetting a monkem by calling them a monkem were virtually nonexistent.

I wish this was easier. I wish I could just lay my hands on your head and transfer what's inside me to you. I wish you could be me, if only for a moment, so you'd know exactly how I feel.

But that's not going to happen, is it?

Wishes never come true.

7

THE SNOW GLOBE

shake it . . .

*   *like this*

It's twelve minutes past three now and I'm back in my room. Still hatted and booted and gloved, still sticky-skinned from the drying cold sweat, and still sick to my bones with fear.

What are you doing, Elliot? Ellamay says, sounding confused and slightly frustrated. *I thought we were ready to go. I thought we'd —*

"It's all right," I tell her. "I've just remembered something, that's all. I won't be a minute."

I cross the room and go into the bathroom.

Oh, right, Ellamay says. *I see.*

She thinks I'm going to the toilet.

"No, it's not that," I tell her, opening the cabinet above the sink. "I'm just checking to make sure there aren't any pills in here that I've forgotten about."

You've already done that.

"I'm double-checking."

You've already done that as well.

"I'm triple-checking then."

There are four empty brown-glass pill bottles in the cabinet. I always keep a few empty ones, just in case I break one or something. And Ellamay's right, I *have* already checked each of them twice. But sometimes I get riddled with doubts — about all kinds of stupid little things — and there's something inside me that won't let me rest until I've hammered those doubts into the ground.

So I check all the bottles again — take one out, shake it

like this

unscrew the cap, look inside, turn it upside down and tap it against my palm . . .

Nothing, empty.

I put the cap back on, place it to one side, take the next bottle out of the cabinet. Shake it

like this

unscrew the cap, look inside . . .

Nothing.

I go through the same process with the other two bottles, but they're both empty too, as I knew they would be.

Satisfied?

"Not yet."

I start removing everything else from the cabinet — packets of pills (for headaches and indigestion), eczema cream, toothpaste, toothbrush — and when the shelves are completely empty, I stand there scanning the dusty emptiness for any specks of yellow, hoping against hope that if I look hard enough I'll find a stray pill. But I don't. So then I reach up and start running my fingers through the dust, feeling around in every little corner of the shelves, every little gap between the shelves and the back of the cupboard, every possible place where a small yellow pill could be lodged . . .

There's nothing there.

No doubt about it.

I close the cabinet, reach into my pocket, and pull out my current pill bottle. I give it a shake

like this

and the last remaining pill rattles thinly against the glass. I close my eyes for a second and think again about taking it now. The last one I took is beginning to wear off, and I can already feel the first faint stirrings of the thing I dread the most — the beast that is the fear of fear itself — and I know that if I don't take the pill now . . .

Save it for later, Ellamay says.

"I don't think I can."

You're probably going to need it later a lot more than you need it now.

I know she's right.

I know I have to wait.

I shake the bottle one more time

like this

and put it back in my pocket.

Is that it? Ellamay says. *Can we go now? It's going to be completely dark outside if we don't go soon.*

"I know," I tell her, crossing over to the bedside table and picking up my flashlight, "that's why I need this."

I switch it on to make sure it's working. I already know that it is—I check it every night, and I put new batteries in it a couple of days ago—but I go ahead and check it anyway.

It works. The beam's strong and bright.

I drop the flashlight into my coat pocket, turn to leave . . .

Then stop.

And slowly turn around.

What now? says Ella.

The snow globe was a gift from Auntie Shirley. She'd been on a day trip to Whitby with her son, Gordon, and when she was looking around one of the souvenir shops, she'd spotted a snow globe that she really liked. In fact, she'd liked it so much that she'd bought two of them—one for herself and one for Mum.

I'd never seen a snow globe before, so when Mum finally showed it to me — after thinking long and hard about whether it would frighten me or not — I had no idea what it was. I remember holding it in my hands and gazing curiously at it, wondering what on earth it could be. A small glass dome, filled with clear liquid, with a miniature woodland scene inside. It was a fairy-tale scene — Little Red Riding Hood walking through the woods with the Big Bad Wolf — and although the small plastic figures and plastic trees weren't particularly well made or anything, there was something about them, something about the whole thing, that felt very special to me.

"Shake it," Mum said, smiling.

I didn't know what she meant.

"Like this," she told me, gesturing with her hand.

I copied her, awkwardly shaking the globe, and I was so surprised when it filled up with a blizzard of tiny snowflakes that I actually cried out in delight.

Mum was so relieved that I wasn't scared of the snow globe, and even more pleased that I actually seemed to like something for a change, that she let me keep it. And it's been sitting on my shelf ever since.

Shirley keeps her snow globe on the windowsill of her living room, and on the few occasions when I've been in her house — visiting with Mum — I've always wondered if there's some kind of connection between our two identical snow globes, some kind of at-a-distance awareness of each other . . .

Or something.

I don't know.

What is it, Elliot? says Ella.

"Nothing," I tell her, looking away from the snow globe.

What did you see?

"What do you mean?"

You know what I mean. What did you see just now in the snow globe?

"Nothing . . ."

She knows I'm lying. She always knows.

Just tell me, she says quietly. *What did you see?*

"It was snowing . . . like someone had shaken it up. That's what made me look at it. And I saw something . . . or I thought I did."

In the snow?

"In the whole thing."

What was it, Elliot? What did you see?

I was in there, in the snow globe. Or something *of* me was in there . . . a bedraggled figure, limping along the pathway through the woods . . . snow falling in the darkness . . . great black trees all around me, their white-topped branches glinting in an unknown light . . . and up ahead of me, an endless climb of rough wooden steps leading up a steep-sided slope . . .

That's what I saw.

It was all there, all in a timeless moment, and then it was gone again, and all that remained of it was an unfamiliar — and unsettling — feeling of deadness in my heart.

8

A Blood-Red Nightmare

I was six when Mum took me to see a child psychologist. I don't think she really wanted me to see one—partly because she knew it would terrify me, and partly because it meant admitting to herself that my problem *was* mental rather than physical, which she still didn't want to accept. But deep down she knew it was true, and she knew she had to do something about it. So she'd asked the Doc to recommend someone, and he'd asked around and come back with a name, and Mum got in touch with her and made an appointment.

We got as far as the waiting room.

When the psychologist (or therapist, or whatever she called herself) came out of her consulting room and called me and Mum in, I simply couldn't move. The sheer sight of her terrified me so much that I went into some kind of shock—paralyzed in my chair, my muscles locked up, my eyes bulging, my throat too tight to breathe. The psychologist lady also froze for a moment, and I could tell by the look on her face that she was a bit startled by my petrified reaction to her. But, to her credit, she composed herself pretty quickly. Forcing a friendly smile to her face, she came over to where I was sitting with Mum and stopped in front of us. I didn't want to look at her, but I just couldn't help it. She was fairly old, but not ancient or anything. She had longish white hair tied back in a braid, and she was wearing a big necklace made out of shiny gold discs. She had a pea-size mole or something on her upper lip, a hard-looking dark-brown lump, and as I sat there staring helplessly at it, I suddenly began to imagine it pulsing and throbbing, turning red, and then I saw it splitting open, and a big fat yellow fly crawling out . . .

"Hello, Elliot," the psychologist lady started to say. "My name's . . ."

I didn't hear the rest of it. I was already up and running for the door, screaming my heart out as I went.

About six months after that, Mum and the Doc arranged for another psychologist to visit me at home, but that didn't work out either. The night before the day of the visit, I got myself into such a state just thinking about it that I ended up being physically ill. Vomiting, diarrhea, cold sweats, a burning fever . . .

The home visit was canceled.

"How about if I talk to him?" the Doc said to Mum. "I could ask him how he feels about everything, why he's so frightened of things, and I could record our conversation, then pass it on to a child psychologist to see what they think."

"Would they be willing to do that?" Mum asked.

"There's no harm in asking, is there?"

DOC: How do you actually feel when you're frightened of something, Elliot?

ME: I feel scared.

DOC: Do you know why?

ME: What do you mean?

DOC: What I'm trying to get at is *why* you get so frightened. What is it that makes you afraid?

ME: It depends.

DOC: On what?

ME: Different things scare me in different ways.

DOC: Can you give me an example?

ME: Like what?

DOC: Cars, for instance. You're frightened of cars, aren't you?

ME: Yeah.

DOC: Why?

ME: Because they can kill me.

DOC: Could you expand on that a bit?

ME: When I'm in a car, all I can think about is what happens if something goes wrong with it and it swerves off the road, or if something goes wrong with the driver and they lose control and drive into a wall, or if something goes wrong with another car or its driver and that car loses control and smashes into us . . . that's why I'm frightened of cars.

DOC: Because you think they can kill you?

ME: Because they *can* kill me.

DOC: So it's a fear based on a possible future reality.

ME: I don't know what that means.

DOC: It means you're frightened of something that *could* happen. It's highly unlikely that it *will* happen, but there's always a possibility.

ME: Right.

DOC: What about when you're scared of things that don't pose an obvious threat? Like colors. What is it about the color red that scares you, for example? Is it the actual color itself?

ME: Not really, no.

DOC: What is it then? Does the color red remind you of something scary?

ME: Blood.

DOC: Blood?

ME: Yeah.

DOC: Red reminds you of blood.

ME: Yeah.

DOC: And that scares you?

ME: Yeah.

DOC: Why?

ME: I don't know . . . it just does. When I see something red, the redness of it just kind of fills my head with blood.

DOC: Is that why you ran away from that Santa Claus when you were little?

It happened eight years ago, when I was five years old. I was in town with Mum, clinging on to her hand as we made our way through the crowds of festive shoppers. It was so noisy and chaotic that I was already scared out of my wits, but that was nothing compared to the utter horror I felt when a hunch-backed Santa Claus suddenly appeared right in front of me.

I don't know where he came from — he was probably part of some Christmas carnival or something — and I don't know what on earth he thought he was doing either. All I know is that as he loomed toward me out of the crowd — stooped over (so his head was level with mine), and with his arms stretched out toward me — I was so shocked and horrified that I actually wet myself. He was hideous. His face all scabby and broken-veined, his eyes unfocused, his teeth just a row of rotten black stubs. His dirty old Santa's beard was yellowed with nicotine stains and dotted with cigarette burns and ketchup drips and God-knows-what-else, and underneath the beard, clearly visible, was a thick growth of bristly black stubble.

Although he had all the Santa gear on — red hat, red jacket, red pants — he didn't look anything like he was supposed to. He wasn't very old for a start — midtwenties at most — and he wasn't fat or jolly either. He was just horrible. A blood-red nightmare. And he smelled bad too, like rotten fruit . . . rotten fruit mixed with cigarette smoke.

It must have been obvious how terrified I was, but as I cowered away from him, desperately hiding behind Mum's legs, he just grinned and kept coming after me, as if it was some kind of game.

"Don't be scared, kid," he said, his voice all wheezy and croaky. "It's only Santa . . . hey, come on, I ain't gonna hurt ya . . ."

This all happened so quickly that I don't think Mum knew what was going on at first, but when this monstrous Santa reached around her legs, pawing at me in what he must have thought was a playful fashion, and I tore my hand from hers and ran off into the crowd, she suddenly sprang into action. When the devil-Santa stood up straight, swore under his breath, and started to come after me, she lashed out at him, kicking him hard in the groin, and as he doubled over in agony and sank to the ground, she ran off after me, calling out my name as she went.

ME: I would have been scared of him whatever color clothes he was wearing.

DOC: Do you think you would have been less scared if he wasn't dressed all in red?

ME: Yeah, but I still would have run away from him.

DOC: What about all the red things you see every day? I mean, that Homer Simpson mug on your desk over there, the one with all your pens in . . . that's got bits of red on it.

ME: I'm okay with *bits* of red. It's only when there's a big solid lump of it that it really gets to me. Like if someone's wearing a red coat or something. And it doesn't happen all the time either.

DOC: What do you mean?

ME: Sometimes I can see the scary colors and they don't do anything to me at all, and other times they only bother me a bit. But on scary-color days . . . that's when it's really bad.

DOC: What other colors are scary?

ME: Black, blue . . . purple sometimes.

DOC: Do they fill your head with frightening things in the same way that red does?

ME: Yeah.

DOC: What does blackness fill your head with?

ME: Death, darkness, night, nothingness . . .

DOC: Blue?

ME: The sea, lakes, and rivers . . .

DOC: What is it about the sea that scares you?

ME: Drowning.

DOC: Do you have scary days and nonscary days with these colors too?

ME: Yeah.

DOC: Different days for different colors?

ME: No. A scary-color day is the same for all colors, and so is a nonscary day.

DOC: What kind of day is it today?

ME: Not too bad. Not completely nonscary, but not totally scary either. Somewhere in between.

DOC: And what about all this, Elliot? All your books, the television, your laptop . . .

ME: What about it?

DOC: Well, a few minutes ago, you were telling me

about your fear of cars, but if the television was on now, you'd almost certainly come across a car on one of the channels. It might be in a film, an advert, a documentary . . . cars are everywhere on the television. So how can you watch it?

ME: It's not real. A car on the television isn't a ton of speeding metal, it's just a digital image made up of millions of pixels. Pixels can't kill you.

DOC: Doesn't it *remind* you of cars though, like red reminds you of blood?

ME: No.

DOC: Why not?

ME: I don't know. That's just how it is. I don't have any control over what scares me and what doesn't.

DOC: Does anything on the television frighten you?

ME: No.

DOC: Not even horrific things on the news?

ME: It's not real.

DOC: It's a representation of reality though, isn't it?

ME: It's still not real.

DOC: And that's the same with all your books and the things you see on the internet, is it? It's not real, so it's not frightening?

ME: I can't explain it. I don't even bother trying to

understand it myself anymore. I just . . . I don't know. I just do my best to live with it.

DOC: Do you ever get used to being scared all the time?

ME: No, but I've kind of become used to not getting used to it.

9

At Least a Million

"Are you sure you can trust her?" Dake asked Jenner.

They'd left the moors behind now and were driving along a narrow road that would eventually bring them out at the top of the village. The snow had eased off a little, and although the icy wind was still blowing hard, the Land Rover was shielded from the worst of it by the high banks and drystone walls on either side of the road.

"I don't trust anyone," Jenner said matter-of-factly.

"So how do you know she's not lying?"

"Because she knows what I'll do to her if she is."

Dake didn't doubt there was a veiled threat to him in Jenner's answer — *and* you'd *better not mess me around either* — and he also knew that Jenner didn't make idle threats. He made promises, and he kept them.

"It just seems a bit odd, that's all," Dake said.

"What do you mean?"

"The timing, you know . . . Christmas and everything. I still don't get it. I mean, you would have thought they'd empty the place over Christmas, not keep it all there."

Jenner sighed. "How many more times do I have to tell you? The whole point of this, the reason it won't be expected — and why we're going to get away with it — is precisely *because* of the timing. They usually *would* keep all the branches empty over Christmas, but when their internal computer system crashed last week, it messed up the program they use to schedule and track the collections —" Jenner paused, glancing sideways at Dake. "Do I really have to go over all this again? Don't you remember *anything,* for God's sake?"

"Yeah, of course I remember," Dake said defensively. "It's just . . . well, you know . . . I can't be expected to remember everything, can I?"

Jenner shook his head in disbelief. He'd always known that Dake wasn't particularly intelligent — he could barely read or write, for a start — but Jenner was beginning to wonder now if there was something seriously wrong with him. How could he *not* remember what he'd already been told at least three or four times?

Jenner slowed the Land Rover and pulled over to let a tractor go by. Once it had passed, he lit a cigarette and turned to Dake.

"The money's there, okay?" he said, as patiently as possible. "It's in the vault. That's all you need to know."

"How much?"

"I've already told you that."

"I know." Dake grinned. "I just want to hear it again."

"At least a million, according to the girl. Probably more."

"At least a million . . ." Dake echoed dreamily.

"Yeah, and the best thing about it is they won't even know it's gone until the day after Boxing Day."

"He'll know though, won't he?"

"Who?"

"The manager guy, you know . . . the one who's going to open the safe for us. He'll know the money's gone."

"He won't tell anyone."

"Why not?"

"Because he'll know what I'll do to his mother if he does."

10

A Dead Black Line

ME: Do you think I'm crazy?

DOC: Do you?

ME: I don't know ... sometimes, maybe. I'm definitely not normal, am I?

DOC: None of us are normal. We all have things wrong with us. It's just that some of those things have a much bigger effect on our lives than others.

ME: Do you think something could have gone wrong in my head when I was a baby?

DOC: Do you mean when your heart stopped?

ME: Yeah. Maybe my brain stopped too, or it got damaged or something.

DOC: Well, that *can* happen, yes. If you're starved of oxygen at birth, it can lead to irreversible brain damage. But in all the instances I've ever come across, the oxygen supply has been stopped for at least two or three minutes, usually quite a bit longer. But that wasn't the case with you, Elliot. Your heart stopped beating for less than a minute.

ME: Yeah, but what if —?

DOC: There's absolutely nothing wrong with your mind, Elliot. Trust me. If you'd suffered any brain damage, I'd know.

ME: So are you saying it's perfectly all right for me to be terrified of everything?

DOC: No, of course not.

ME: So there *is* something wrong with my brain.

Sometimes I have no sense of the present. All I can feel is a sense of the past and a sense of the future — the "then" and the "when." I can look back and remember things — things that happened, things that I did — and I can look forward to things that haven't happened yet. I can imagine things happening in the future — the next half hour, the next day, next Monday afternoon, next year. I can do all that. But the present . . . the present seems to pass me by. I can't get hold of it. It's like a shapeless and senseless void that moves, like a cursor, between the past and the future. A dead black line, forever moving, forever being . . . but never actually there.

*

ME: I know you think I'm weird.

DOC: What makes you say that?

ME: I heard you talking to Mum once. You told her it was really weird how sometimes I sound really grown-up, almost like an adult, but other times I seem almost babyish.

DOC: I didn't say it was "really weird," I just said I'd noticed it, that's all. And I didn't say "babyish" either. All I said was that sometimes the way you talk makes you sound older than you are, and sometimes you come across as being younger than you are. I didn't say it was "weird." And I wouldn't use that word anyway.

ME: What word would you use?

DOC: I don't know . . . "different," perhaps. "Unusual." There's nothing wrong with being unusual.

I've never met my father. According to Mum, she met him at a party, they spent the night together, and that was that. They never saw each other again.

"It was all perfectly amiable," she told me once. "He was a lovely man, and we had a very nice time together. But neither of us wanted to take it any further, and we were both quite happy to go our separate ways."

"What was his name?" I asked her.

"Martyn."

"Martyn what?"

"I honestly don't know. He introduced himself as Martyn, and I told him I was Grace, and that's all we needed to know."

Even if she had known his last name, she still wouldn't have made any effort to contact him when she found out she was pregnant.

"It would only have complicated things," she explained. "And besides, apart from his name, the only other thing I knew about Martyn was that he lived in Los Angeles and he was a writer, but he didn't write under his real name. So I couldn't have tracked him down even if I'd wanted to, which I didn't."

I don't miss having a father — you can't miss what you've never had, can you? — and on the rare occasions when I do wonder what it would be like to have a dad, the mere thought of it makes me shudder. A man living in my house? A monkem? A man I'd have to share Mum with . . . ?

No.

I wouldn't like that one bit.

DOC: We might not know the precise cause of your problem, Elliot, but we know how it affects you, and it might be possible to lessen those effects to some degree.

ME: How?

DOC: There are antianxiety medications that might help. They're obviously not intended for treating the level of fear that afflicts you, and normally I'd never even consider this type of medication for a child, but you're a far from normal case, Elliot.
ME: Thanks a lot.

The Doc looks totally different when he smiles, which isn't very often. But when he does smile, it lightens his face, makes him look younger. It lifts his mask of somber gravity and reveals a twinkle of the child in him.

DOC: Anyway, I've talked to your mum about it, and although she hates the idea of putting you on medication as much as I do, she agrees that it's worth trying. But only if you want to.
ME: Will the drugs stop me being afraid?
DOC: No, but they might lessen the severity of your fears.
ME: So I'll still be scared of things, but not so much.
DOC: Possibly, yes. It's also possible that medication won't help you at all. In fact, it could actually make you feel worse. But the only way to find out is by trying it. You also need to bear in mind that there are dozens of different types of antianxiety medication,

and it could easily take months, or even years, to find out which of them — if any — is best for you. Now I know this is a lot to think about, but at the moment, that's all I want you to do — just think about it, okay? There's no rush. You can take as much time as you want. And if there's anything you're not sure about, anything you want to ask, just let me know, okay?

ME: Yeah.

DOC: We can do this, Elliot. We can do everything possible to make you better. But we have to do it together. We have to do it between the three of us — you, your mum, and me.

And Ellamay, I added silently.

Thank you, she said.

You're welcome.

11

MY EVERY DAY AND NIGHT

It's twenty-one minutes past three now, and I'm back in the hallway, making some final adjustments to my Wellington boots. They're actually the Doc's boots. He left them at our house once — I don't know why — and they've been here ever since. They're far too big for me, which is why I've had to customize them by stuffing the toe ends with scrunched-up newspaper. I used to have my own pair of Wellingtons, but it's been so many years since I wore them — so many years since I've needed them — that I don't have a clue where they are. In fact, it's quite possible that Mum got rid of them a long time ago. And even if she didn't, and I did know where they are, they'd be at least a couple of sizes too small for me by now.

I don't feel very comfortable in the Doc's Wellingtons, but they're the only boots I could find, so I don't really have much choice.

The gloves and the coat and the hat I'm wearing aren't mine either. They're Mum's. As with the boots, I used to have my own coat and everything, but if you barely ever leave the house — and I barely ever leave my room, let alone the house — there's not much point in having outdoor clothing. And besides, I can always borrow Mum's if I need to. She's only a bit bigger than me, so they're not too bad a fit.

Although, having said that . . .

What are you doing now? Ellamay says.

"These gloves are a bit loose. I'm just going to try padding them out a bit with a few scraps of wadded-up newspaper. It won't take long."

That's enough, Elliot.

"What?"

We have to go. You can't keep putting it off.

"I'm not —"

Yes, you are. You know you are.

She's right, of course. I keep trying to convince myself that I'm ready to do this, that I've got my fear under control . . . but the truth is, I'm as terrified now as I was twenty-one minutes ago. All I want to do is go back to the sanctuary of my room and stay there forever. It's the only place I feel safe, the only place I ever want to be. My room.

My everything.

My world.

*

The countryside can be a scary place when darkness falls. Before I had my own specially modified fear-proof room, I'd often lie awake at night just waiting for the horror-sounds to begin. The piercing screech of an owl, the scream of a fox (like someone in terrible pain), the pitiful cries of rabbits being killed . . . and monkem noises too — gunshots from night hunters, the shattering roar of a speeding car or motorbike, drunk monkems passing by, shouting and laughing. And on top of all that, there's the constant sound of army maneuvers up on the moors — the distant pop-popping of gunfire, the rumble of tanks, soldiers' war cries, the whiz-bang of flares going off . . .

And even when the night *is* silent, it's a silence of darkness and dread, a silence that's always waiting for the next unholy scream.

But I don't hear anything of the night anymore.

My fear-proof room is one hundred percent soundproof.

I don't know exactly how it works, but basically the walls and the ceiling are made up of several layers of various kinds of stuff that either absorbs or reflects sound, and the only window is quadruple glazed. The window looks out over the fields at the back of the house, but I very rarely actually see them because there's a blackout blind that totally obscures the view. I can raise the blind if I want to — and occasionally I find the courage to have a quick look—but most of the time it stays down, shielding me from the outside world.

The room's painted white all over. I chose white because for me it's the color that comes closest to nothing. It's the most nonscary color, the color that doesn't fill my head or my heart with anything. I can lie on my bed staring up at the ceiling, sometimes for hours on end, and I don't have to worry about the sky of whiteness invading my thoughts and feelings. It leaves me alone . . .

It leaves *us* alone.

Me and Ellamay.

Solitude becomes us.

My room has everything I need. I've got my own bathroom— shower, sink, toilet . . . but no bath. Baths are too scary. You can drown in a bath. I've got a kettle and cups and stuff, so I can make myself a hot drink whenever I want (tea or hot chocolate only—coffee makes me twitch and shake like a crazy thing). I've got a little fridge (cold drinks, milk, yogurt, butter), and a little kitchen area with plates and cutlery and a bread box, so I can have a sandwich or something whenever I feel like it. I've got a bed, of course, and all my own furniture—settee, armchair, desk. I've got a laptop, a twenty-four-inch flat-screen TV, a landline phone, and a cell phone. The landline is set up so it only receives incoming calls from Mum (and instead of ringing, a green light flashes on and off when she calls), and the cell phone is for emergencies only.

I've got all the clothes I need in here, which isn't a lot, and I've got all my "school" stuff too — pens, notebooks, textbooks. (Mum tried her best to get me into the local school, but after two disastrous attempts — both of which traumatized me for weeks — she accepted that normal schooling was out of the question for me, and since then she's taught me herself at home.)

Most important of all, I've got all my "nonschool books" in here too, the books I just like reading. Two walls of my room are completely taken up with bookshelves, and the shelves are packed solid with hundreds of books. I don't know exactly how many I've got, but the last time I counted them — just over a year ago — the total was 1,762.

So that's it, basically.

That's my world.

My sanctuary.

My every day and night.

12

THE MOTHER

Jenner glanced at his watch again.

It was 12:28.

They were parked across the road from the house, and so far, things hadn't been going quite as Jenner had planned. For a start, he hadn't given any consideration to the possibility that the mother might not be at home, so when they'd arrived at the house twenty minutes ago and seen that her car wasn't there, it had completely thrown Jenner off balance. And for another thing, once he'd decided that the only thing to do was wait and hope the mother came back soon, he'd begun to realize that maybe their Santa Claus outfits weren't such a good idea after all. As disguises, plain and simple, they were excellent. No one who saw them in their Santa gear could possibly give a meaningful description of them. Unfortunately, no one who saw two cheap-and-nasty Santas sitting in a parked Land Rover would ever forget them either, especially if they'd tried making conversation with them, which several curious passersby had already done.

But there was no point in worrying about it, Jenner told himself. It was what it was, and there was nothing they could do about it. And besides . . .

"About bloody time," he said as a silvery-gray Volvo pulled into the driveway.

"Is that her?" Dake asked.

"Of course it's her. Who else is it going to be?"

"I don't know, do I?"

Jenner watched as the mother got out of the car and scurried over to the front door, digging into her handbag as she went, looking — no doubt — for the door key.

"She's left it running," Dake said.

"What?"

"The car . . . she's left it running."

13

MOLOXETINE

My fear pills are a drug called Moloxetine. It's not a commonly prescribed medication, and I only ended up taking it after the Doc had tried me on just about every other antianxiety drug he could think of. None of the others had been right for me. Some of them just hadn't worked at all, and others had helped a little bit, but not enough to outweigh their sometimes quite drastic side effects — hallucinations, mania, aggression, extreme fatigue, hyperactivity, acute diarrhea, vomiting, panic attacks, severe depression, suicidal thoughts . . .

As I said to the Doc once, "I'd rather be terrified all the time for the rest of my life than wake up every morning wanting to kill myself."

My fear pills don't stop me being scared. I still live in constant fear, and my life is still ruled by that fear, but with Moloxetine . . . well, it's hard to describe exactly what it does for me, but basically it makes everything feel not quite so terrible. Of course, there's a massive difference between feeling "not quite so terrible" and feeling "good," or "okay," or "not too bad," but the way I see it is that any relief, no matter how small, is a lot better than nothing. It's like offering a coat to a naked person caught outside on a rainy winter's day. The coat's not going to solve their problem, it's not going to stop them being cold and wet, but they'd have to be pretty stupid to not wear it.

The very worst of my fears, the thing I dread more than anything else, is the fear of fear itself. It's a truly monstrous thing, like a howling demon whirling around inside me, an insatiable beast that keeps getting bigger and bigger all the time . . . bigger, faster, stronger, hungrier. It feeds on itself, so the bigger it gets, the more it needs to eat, and the more it eats, the bigger it gets . . . and if it isn't kept under control, it can end up dragging me, screaming, to the very edge of my sanity.

Moloxetine helps to keep the beast at bay. I know it's still there. I can hear it sometimes, a distant low growl, and every now and then I can taste the foul odor of its demonic breath creeping into the back of my throat. But as long as I keep taking my fear pills — six a day at regular intervals, regardless of how I'm feeling — the beast doesn't get any closer. But if I'm late taking a pill, or I completely forget to take one — which usually only happens when I'm feeling so (relatively) good that I can't (or don't want to) have anything to do with *not* feeling good . . . when that happens, the beast comes back with a vengeance.

It's as if it's there all the time, skulking around inside me, locked in a cage of Moloxetine's making, just waiting . . . waiting . . . waiting for its chance to escape and come after me. And if the Moloxetine begins to wear off for any reason, the lock on the cage begins to weaken, and the longer I go without the drug, the weaker the cage becomes — the lock cracks and crumbles, the door swings open . . .

The insatiable beast is set free.

Which is why it's so important that I never run out of pills.

Because if I do, I have to face the beast.

"It's coming, Ella. It's getting closer. I can smell its breath."

Me too.

"It stinks."

It's only a smell, Elliot. It can't hurt you.

"Yeah, but the beast can hurt me. It's hungry. I need to put it back in its cage before it's too late. I *need* the last pill, Ella. I need to take it now."

Silence . . . the silence of Ellamay's thinking.

Then, *All right. Take it. We'll just have to hope that we find Mum and Shirley sooner rather than later.*

"And that they've got my prescription."

Yeah.

I take the pill bottle from my pocket, shake it

like this

then I unscrew the cap and carefully tip the last remaining
pill into the (slightly cupped) palm of my hand.

Make sure you don't drop it, Ella says.

"Yeah, right . . . like I hadn't already thought of that myself."

She gives me an imaginary slap on the back of my head.

"Hey! I almost *did* drop it then."

Sorry.

I pop the pill in my mouth and swallow it dry.

Bye-bye for now, Mr. Beastie . . .

Bye-bye.

14

LET'S GET THIS DONE

"She's left it running," Dake said.

"What?"

"The car . . . she's left it running."

He was right, Jenner realized. Clouds of blue-gray exhaust smoke were still chugging out into the icy cold air, and as Jenner wound down his window, he could hear the low rumble of the idling engine.

He switched his attention to the mother, watching her as she opened the front door, shook the snow from her coat, and went inside. Jenner waited, staring hard at the still-open door.

"She's left the door —"

"I know."

There was no mistaking the signs. Leaving the car running, leaving the front door open . . . she wasn't home for good. She was just stopping off for some reason. And any second now, she'd be coming back out and getting back into the car . . .

Jenner looked at his watch.

It was 12:31.

"All right," he said, opening the car door. "Let's get this done."

15

The Snarl of the Beast

It happened like this.

I have a renewable prescription for my fear pills, which basically means that instead of having to make an appointment with the Doc every time I need more Moloxetine, Mum or Shirley just hands in a duplicate prescription slip at the pharmacy in town. The pharmacy then sends it to the Doc's office to be authorized, a doctor signs it (not necessarily the Doc), then it goes back to the pharmacy and they get it ready for collection. Each time it's picked up I get a new prescription slip for another month's worth of Moloxetine, and three weeks later, the process starts all over again.

We have to allow two working days to get the prescription, and we always put the request in at least a week before I'm due to run out of pills, so even if there is some kind of holdup, I still have enough Moloxetine to keep me going.

On the day before Christmas Eve (Thursday), I had six pills left of my last prescription, and another full bottle that Mum had picked up the week before. So I had more than enough pills to get me through Christmas and into the New Year, and there shouldn't have been anything to worry about. And there wasn't . . .

Until I opened the new bottle.

It was two o'clock in the afternoon, and I was in my bathroom, taking my third pill of the day. While I was there, I thought I might as well transfer the last six tablets to the new bottle. So I took it off the shelf, opened it up, and was just about to empty the old bottle into it when something caught my eye. The pills . . . the pills in the new bottle . . . they didn't look right. I looked closer, peering into the bottle. The pills in there *were* small and yellow, like Moloxetine, but they weren't quite the same. They were just a bit too small, a bit too yellow.

Unless . . .

Unless.

Maybe the pills had been redesigned. Maybe the company that makes Moloxetine had decided it was time to give them a new look. It was possible, wasn't it? It didn't make much sense to me — what's the point of redesigning a pill? — but it wasn't out of the question.

I looked at the label on the bottle. I couldn't make out the writing at first because my hand was shaking so much — as was the rest of me — and the only way I could read the label was by putting the bottle down on the counter beside the sink and leaning in close to it.

The wording on the label was exactly the same as it always is.

168 Moloxetine 50 mg Tabs
Take ONE six times a day

I picked up the bottle again and shakily tipped out a couple of pills onto the counter. Now that they were out of the brown glass bottle it was even more obvious how different they were. The yellow was totally wrong. And although they were only a bit smaller than they should be, their overall shape was nothing like my usual pills. My usual pills are kind of saucer-shaped. These were much flatter, like little disks.

I was still clinging to the possibility that there was nothing to worry about, that these pills were just the same old Moloxetine with a brand-new look, but even as I leaned down over the counter for a really close look at the pills I'd tipped out, I knew I was just clutching at straws.

I could feel the truth inside me, and it didn't feel good.

And when I read the brand name printed on the new tablets, my gut feeling was confirmed.

Mectazone, it said.

Not **Moloxetine**.

Mectazone.

I straightened up and took a few steadying breaths, trying unsuccessfully to control my racing heart, then I went over to my desk, opened my laptop, and googled "mectazone."

Mectazone, Wikipedia said, *is a proton pump inhibitor that decreases the amount of acid in the stomach. Mectazone is used to treat symptoms of gastroesophageal reflux disease . . .*

I didn't know what a "proton pump inhibitor" was, and I didn't know what "gastroesophageal reflux disease" was either, but it didn't make the slightest bit of difference. The only thing that mattered was that these pills, all 168 of them, *weren't* Moloxetine. I'd been given the wrong prescription. Which meant that I only had six fear pills left.

Six . . .

Enough to last me until this time tomorrow.

I could feel it now . . .

The beast.

Deep inside me.

I could feel it beginning to stir.

Mum couldn't believe it when I told her what had happened.

"They're supposed to *check* it, for God's sake," she said,

glaring at the bottle in her hand. "In fact, it's supposed to be checked *twice,* by two people. Look . . ."

She showed me the label, pointing out two little boxes in the top right-hand corner. One was marked *DISP,* the other *CH.* Both boxes had been initialed; both sets of initials were different.

"They've *both* initialed to say they checked it," Mum went on, getting angrier by the second, "but they can't have, otherwise they would have spotted the mistake." She shook her head again. "It's *unbelievable* . . . it really is. I mean, what if you hadn't noticed? What if you'd started taking the wrong medication? God knows what could have happened . . ."

She was right, of course. It *was* unbelievable, and it was perfectly natural for her to be angry. But one of the things about fear that makes it so powerful is that it totally over-whelms everything else — other feelings, other emotions — and although I was angry too, my fear was a hundred times stronger. The fear of running out of pills. The fear of fear itself. The fear of the beast.

So all I cared about then — as Mum carried on ranting and cursing — the *only* thing I was thinking about, was getting more Moloxetine.

I had six pills left.

It was Christmas Eve tomorrow. After that, the pharmacy

would be closed for two days. If I didn't get a new prescription by this time tomorrow . . .

No.

It was too gut-wrenching to think about.

"Mum?" I said.

Her eyes were still burning with anger as she turned to me, but almost immediately she recognized the look on my face— the look of fear—and she knew at once what I needed her to do.

"I'll call the pharmacy right now," she said. "We'll get this figured out, okay?"

"Right," she said, after she'd called the pharmacy, "I've spoken to the senior pharmacist, and everything's all right. She was very apologetic about the mistake, and they're going to give us a new prescription for Moloxetine."

The snarl of the beast immediately began to fade.

I could still hear it though.

Just as I could hear the slight hesitation in Mum's voice. It sounded to me like there was a "but" or a "however" coming.

And I was right.

"The only thing is," Mum went on, "the pharmacy has to physically see the wrongly issued bottle of pills before they can give us a new prescription. Which means I'm going to have to go down there this afternoon."

"Yeah, but you're going to have to go down to pick up the new prescription anyway, aren't you?"

"Well, yes . . . but not today."

I frowned. "Why not?"

"They don't have any Moloxetine in stock. They checked with the other local pharmacies, but none of them have any either. So they had to put in an emergency order for it." Mum paused, giving me a worried look. I could feel the blood draining from my skin, and I guessed she could see it. "It's okay, love," she said, putting her arms around me. "It'll be there first thing tomorrow morning."

Yeah, but what if it's not? I couldn't help thinking. *What if the delivery van gets stuck in the snow or breaks down or something? What if the driver gets sick, or the van crashes? What if I don't get my pills tomorrow?*

"Everything's going to be fine, Elliot," Mum said, quietly but firmly. She put her hands on my shoulders and looked me in the eye. "I know this is really hard for you, but you *will* get your prescription tomorrow. You have enough Moloxetine for today, don't you?"

"Yeah . . ."

"And enough for tomorrow morning."

I nodded.

"Trust me," she said. "It's going to be all right. Okay?"

I nodded again.

It was all I could do.

Whenever Mum has to go out, she normally asks Shirley or the Doc to stay in the house with me. But that afternoon, they were both unavailable. Shirley was in York, doing some last-minute Christmas shopping, and the Doc was out of the country. Once a year, he does volunteer work overseas, providing medical care wherever it's needed. This time he was helping out in a refugee camp in Lebanon. He usually stays away for at least a month, so he wouldn't be back until the end of January.

"I'll be okay on my own, Mum," I told her.

"Are you sure?"

"You won't be long, will you?"

She shook her head. "Half an hour at the most."

"I'll be okay."

I stayed in my room while Mum drove down to the pharmacy to show them the wrong bottle of pills.

I wasn't okay.

I could feel the beast pacing around in its cage now.

Its moment was coming.

It was ready . . .

Ready and waiting.

In twenty-four hours, it would have me.

I couldn't think about it. All I could do was lie on my bed, curled up into a ball, with Ellamay curled up beside me.

16

ONE, TWO, THREE

I wasn't too bad for the rest of the night. When Mum came back from the pharmacy, she assured me again that my prescription would be there first thing in the morning, and as long as I forced myself to believe her — and forced myself to ignore the part of me that couldn't believe her — I just about managed to keep the worst of the sickening fear at bay. That's not to say that I didn't feel terrible, because I did. I was fear-sick all the time. Everything hurt. My head was a mess. I was all cramped up inside . . .

But I was managing.

Just about.

I was coping with it.

At just past midnight though, when I was getting ready for bed, everything suddenly caught up with me.

I was in the bathroom, and I'd just taken my last fear pill of the day. Before putting the bottle back on the shelf, I carefully tipped out the remaining pills and counted them. I'd already counted them at least a dozen times, so I knew exactly how many were left, but I also knew that if I didn't count them again, I wouldn't be able to rest.

So I counted them.

One, two, three . . .

Three.

I don't know why it happened at that particular moment rather than at any other time, but it did, and it was awful. A sudden pain gripped my belly and a lurch of nausea welled up inside me. As I bent over the sink and threw up, the knot of pain in my stomach got worse, twisting and tightening like a belt of barbed wire, and when I heaved again — barely bringing anything up — it hurt so much that I doubled over and fell to my knees, and for the next few minutes, I just knelt there on the floor and retched, emptily and agonizingly, over and over again. The sheer strain of it sent a dizzying surge of blood to my head that made the room spin around and around, and when the retching finally stopped, and I tried to stand up — irrationally thinking it'd make me feel better — the floor tilted beneath my feet, and I staggered backward and stumbled over, cracking my head against the wall.

The next thing I knew, Mum was calling out to me from the other side of the bathroom door.

"Are you all right in there, Elliot? Elliot? Can you hear me? Is everything all right?"

"Uh, yeah . . ." My voice was a feeble croak (and the back of my head was throbbing like hell). I cleared my throat and tried again. "Yeah, I'm okay, Mum . . . I just . . . I won't be a minute, all right?"

An hour or so later, as I lay in bed, staring up at the ceiling, I tried to picture the moment tomorrow morning when Mum would come back from the pharmacy and put the bottle of pills in my hand. I tried to imagine the feel of the glass, the rattle of the pills as I shook the bottle

like this

and the familiar sharp *clack* as I unscrewed the plastic top.

But no matter how hard I tried, willing the feelings to come to me, I just couldn't do it.

As I closed my eyes and tried to sleep, I could hear the mocking laughter of the beast.

17

KAYLEE

Her name was Kaylee Adams. She was twenty-one years old, and she'd worked at the bank since leaving school. She'd met Jenner a few months ago in a local pub. Her friends had warned her to stay away from him — he was a villain, a crook, he'd done time in prison — but that was precisely what Kaylee found attractive about him. She liked "bad boys." She liked flirting with danger. She liked the thrill of it all.

The only thing Jenner liked about Kaylee was the fact that she worked in the bank. He didn't find her particularly good-looking, or even good company, and he positively despised her pretentious attraction to him. He knew exactly what he was to her — a bored girl's plaything — and although that sickened him, he was happy to take full advantage of it.

Kaylee had told him all about Gordon, as she always (sneeringly) called him. She'd told Jenner that although Gordon was almost thirty years old, he still lived at home with his mother, and she still treated him like a little boy.

"She's always calling him at work to ask him stupid questions," Kaylee said, "like what he wants for dinner, or did he remember to take his scarf and gloves with him this morning, stuff like that . . . it's pathetic."

Maybe it is, thought Jenner, *but it's a lot better than having a mother who was so messed up on drink and drugs when you were a baby that she regularly forgot to feed you, and quite often didn't change your nappy for days, and didn't even put up a fight when social services finally took you away from her . . .*

"What about the father?" Jenner asked Kaylee.

She shook her head. "I don't know . . . he doesn't live with them, I know that, but I don't know anything else about him. Gordon's never even mentioned him."

"So it's just the two of them in the house."

"Yeah."

Kaylee had gone on to assure Jenner that on Christmas Eve Gordon would be back home by one o'clock at the latest.

"The bank closes at twelve," she explained. "Then most of us are going to the King's Head for a few drinks. It's kind of a Christmas tradition."

"Does Gordon go with you?"

"Only for about ten minutes, thank God. He forces himself to make an appearance—he thinks it's good for staff morale—but once he's bought the first round of drinks, and taken a microscopic sip from his half pint of lager and lime, he makes his excuses and leaves us to it."

"So what time is it by then?"

Kaylee shrugged. "About twelve thirty. He's got to walk back to the bank to pick up his car, which is another five or ten minutes—"

"Then another ten minutes to drive home."

"Yeah."

"So he's back by one."

"Yeah."

"As long as he doesn't stay longer in the pub, or do some Christmas shopping in town, or stop off in Costa for a cup of coffee and a grilled cheese sandwich . . ."

Kaylee laughed.

"What?" said Jenner.

"Well, for a start, Gordon doesn't drink coffee. It doesn't *agree* with him, apparently. The only thing he drinks is tea from a flask that his mummy makes for him. And as for Christmas shopping . . ." Kaylee shook her head. "He will have done it all months ago. And he *never* stays longer in the pub." She shrugged. "He's Gordon—you can set your watch by him."

Let's just hope you're right, Jenner thought, smiling at her. *For your sake.*

73

18

THE LONESOME RATTLE

Nine o'clock in the morning, Christmas Eve.

The snow was falling heavily, the sky low and dark with thick black clouds, and the wind was getting wilder by the minute.

Mum had called the pharmacy, and they'd confirmed my prescription was there, and now we were in my room, and Mum was ready to go.

Coat, hat, boots, gloves . . .

Car keys in her hand.

She'd told me last night that she was going to call Shirley and ask her to come down and stay with me while she went to the pharmacy, but I'd told her not to bother, that I'd be okay on my own again.

"Are you sure?" she'd asked me.

"Yeah."

The truth was that if Shirley was here she'd want to talk to me, which normally I don't mind at all — I really like talking to her — but today wasn't a normal day. It was hard enough talking to Mum and Ellamay today, let alone anyone else. I needed the silence of solitude.

"I'll be as quick as I can," Mum said. "Okay?"

I nodded . . .

"Are you sure you're all right on your own?"

I nodded again, and again . . .

I couldn't seem to stop nodding my head.

Mum cupped my face in her hands and held me gently, steadying the manic movement of my head.

"Okay?" she murmured after a while.

"Yeah."

I smiled at her, trying to show her that I *was* okay, but I got the feeling — partly from the look in her eyes, and partly from an image that had suddenly appeared in my head — that my smiling face was a grinning skull.

Mum kissed the skull.

"Stay in here, all right?" she told it. "I'll see you in half an hour."

Thirty seconds after she'd left, I opened my door, went down the hallway, and stood by the front door. The double garage (where Mum keeps her car) is no more than ten yards away from the front door, so when I put my ear to the door and listened hard, straining to hear above the gusting wind, I could just about make out the metallic screech of the garage door opening. A few moments later, I heard the *chunk* of the driver's door being pulled shut . . . then another short pause . . . and then finally the whir of the engine starting up . . .

And then, almost immediately, the sound of it spluttering and dying.

Mum tried it again.

The ignition whirred, the engine whined — *yurr-yurr-yurr, yurr-yurr-yurr, yurr-yurr-yurr, yurr, yurr-yurr-yurr* — then it coughed once, rattled, and stopped again.

I heard someone laughing then, and the sound of it made my skin crawl. And then I realized it was me.

Mum tried the engine again.

Yurr-yurr-yurr, yurr-yurr-yurr, yurr-yurr-yurr, yurr, yurr-yurr-yurr . . .

The *yurring* was getting weaker now, and when it stopped this time, there was no cough or rattle, just a hopeless-sounding whine.

I heard the car door opening, then a creak as Mum opened the hood, and then everything went quiet.

After ten minutes or so, I heard the slam of the hood closing, the *chunk* of the driver's door, and then the sound of Mum trying the ignition again. This time it didn't even whine. It just made a dull *clonk*.

*

Mum's gloves were covered in oil and grease when she came back in, and her face was streaked with black smudges. She must have realized right away that I'd heard her trying (and failing) to start the car, because the first thing she said when she came through the door was, "It's all right, Elliot, nothing to worry about. Everything's okay." She shut the door and started taking her coat off. "Shirley's going to pick up your prescription," she explained. "I just called her. She's on her way to Northallerton at the moment, but all she has to do when she gets there is collect a Christmas present that she ordered last week. Once she's done that, she'll drive right back to town and get your prescription." Mum looked at me. "She won't be long. An hour, hour and a half at the very most."

I tried to hide my disappointment, but Mum knows me too well to be fooled. And it works the other way around too, which was why I knew that she was slightly annoyed with me for being disappointed.

"The car won't start, Elliot," she said, unable to keep a hint of irritation from her voice. "I can't do anything about that right now. And the only other options I have are walking downtown to get your prescription, which I'd rather not do in this weather, or getting a taxi, and they're all going to be really busy today, so I'd probably have to wait hours for one anyway, by which time —"

"Sorry, Mum," I said quietly. "I didn't mean to upset you."

She paused, looking at me, then she let out a long sigh. "I know you didn't, love. And I'm sorry too. It's just . . . well, you know . . ." She smiled sadly. "We could have done without this today, couldn't we?"

I did my best to smile back at her, but it was a pretty feeble attempt. My mouth seemed to have forgotten how to do it.

"Listen," Mum said, "I'll try the car again in a few minutes, okay? And if it still doesn't start —"

"It's all right, Mum," I told her. "You don't have to do that. I'm okay waiting for Shirley."

"Really?"

I nodded. "I've still got two pills left, so even if she's a bit late, I'll still be all right."

"Are you sure?"

"Yeah, honestly, it's not a problem."

She smiled at me.

"You need a wash," I told her. "You've got black stuff all over your face."

At 10:15, I took my second fear pill of the day.

Then, out of habit, I shook the bottle.

The lonesome rattle of the last remaining pill sank me to my knees. *Yeah, honestly, it's not a problem . . .*

My eyes filled with tears, and I broke down and sobbed like a baby.

At 10:47, Shirley called. She was on her way back now, she told Mum, but there were long delays near Brompton-on-Swale because of a serious car accident. She didn't know how much longer she'd be, but she'd let us know as soon as she was on the move again.

"At least she's not far from town," Mum said, trying to be optimistic. "Once she gets going again, it won't take her long to get here."

I just nodded, not trusting myself to speak. I'd put my brave face back on after I'd finally stopped crying, but it was getting harder and harder to keep it on now, and I didn't think I could do it much longer.

11:31.

Mum called Shirley.

The call went to straight to voice mail — *please leave a message after the beep.*

"It's me," Mum said into the phone. "Just checking to see what's happening. Call me as soon as you can, okay?"

She ended the call and turned to me. "The reception's not very good out that way. I'll try her again in a few minutes."

11:38.

Mum got Shirley's voice mail again.

11:49.

And again.

12:04.

And again.

12:16.

Shirley finally called. She was on the move again, just coming into town. She'd see us in twenty minutes.

Mum smiled at me. "All right?"

"Yeah," I said, almost managing a smile.

The snarl of the beast was fading again.

I could still hear it though.

And I knew it wouldn't fall silent until the fear pills were in my hand.

By 12:45, Shirley still hadn't arrived.

When Mum called her this time, her phone didn't even go to voice mail. All Mum got was an automated message. *This person's phone is currently unavailable. Please try again later or send a text.*

Mum frowned, then tried again.

She got the same message.

She called the pharmacy. They told her that Shirley had collected my prescription half an hour ago.

"I know what it'll be," Mum said, ending the call and glancing at her watch. "When I first spoke to Shirley earlier, she said she was going to take the back way to the village so she could stop at her house to pick up our Christmas presents and bring them down to us with your pills. I asked her to come straight here instead. She said she would, but I bet you she stopped there anyway."

Mum didn't sound very convinced, and I guessed she was thinking — as I was — that it wouldn't take Shirley half an hour to stop and pick up some presents, and even if it did, that didn't explain why she wasn't answering her phone.

"I'll try her landline," Mum said.

She called the number, put the phone to her ear, listened for a few moments, then frowned again.

"What is it?" I asked.

"Hold on . . ."

She redialed, listened again, then shook her head.

"That's odd," she said.

"What?"

"It's not ringing. There's no answering machine or anything. The line's just dead."

She thought about it for a few moments, then went over to our landline and picked up the handset. She keyed in a number and put the phone to her ear, then nodded to herself and put it back in the cradle again.

"Ours isn't working either," she said. "The phone lines must be down."

She glanced at her watch.

It was just past one o'clock.

Mum was really worried now, and I knew what she was thinking. Something must have happened to Shirley. Maybe her car had broken down or was stuck in the snow on the way back to the village, or maybe she'd been involved in an accident of some kind, or she'd suddenly been taken ill, and no one had been able to let Mum know because the phone lines were down . . .

Or maybe . . .

No.

There was no point in guessing.

I took a deep breath, closed my eyes for a moment, then said what I had to say.

"You have to go up there, Mum. You have to go up to Shirley's house to find out what's going on."

Mum looked at me. "What makes you think Shirley's at home? She could be anywhere."

"I know, but you have to start looking for her somewhere, don't you? And your car's broken down, don't forget, which means you'll be walking, so it makes sense to check out the closest place first."

Mum thought about that for a while, staring at the floor and nodding quietly to herself, then I saw her go still, and a few seconds later she sighed and shook her head.

"I can't," she muttered, looking up at me. "I can't leave you here on your own, not now. You're almost out of pills. What if—"

"I've got two pills left," I lied. "I'll be all right for hours yet."

"I thought you were down to your last one?"

"So did I, but I found another one in an old pill bottle at the back of the cabinet. And it doesn't matter anyway." I tried a smile. "Once you've found Shirley, I'll have tons of pills."

"But what if I *don't* find her? What if I get to her house and she's not there? What are we going to do then?"

"We'll deal with that if it comes to it," I said.

My voice, and my words, sounded so alien to me that for a moment or two I felt really strange. It was as if I'd become a different person, a different me, and the real me was somehow floating in the air above this other-me, looking down at him. It only lasted a few seconds though, and when I came back to myself—and took a few calming breaths—I felt comparatively normal again.

Keep going, Elliot, Ellamay said. *You're almost there.*

"What are you waiting for, Mum?" I heard myself say. "Just go."

83

*

Ten minutes later, after Mum was all bundled up again — coat, hat, boots, gloves — and after we'd double-checked that our cell phones were working, and agreed on a plan to keep in touch, and after Mum had given me one last hug before opening the door and stepping out into the snow . . . after all that, I finally let go of the relatively self-controlled me that I'd been forcing myself to be for Mum's sake, and as I let out a long sigh of relief and let myself slump down to the floor, it was almost a pleasure to be the real me again, the hopelessly scared-to-death me.

Hello again, Mr. Beastie.

Welcome back.

19

527 YARDS

The plan I'd agreed with Mum was that she'd call me on my cell phone every five minutes — to make sure that I was okay and to let me know that she was okay — and that she'd also call me when she got to Shirley's, no matter what she found when she got there.

The first phone call went ahead almost as planned.

"Elliot?"

"Mum?"

"Can you . . . *shhhkkorr* . . . me?"

"What?"

". . . *kahshhh* . . . you *hear* me?"

The connection kept going crackly and cutting out, and Mum was having to shout to make herself heard above the roar of the wind as well, so I could only make out parts of what she was saying.

"... *shhhkkorr* ... you okay?"

"Yeah. Where are you?"

"... *shhhkkk* ... *kaaahh* ... *kahshhh* ... village ..."

"What?"

"... go now ... *kaaahh* ... signal ... *kahshhh* ... later ..."

"What? Mum? Are you there? Hello?"

She'd gone.

We'd spoken to each other, though, that was the main thing. We'd let each other know we were okay. And now all I had to do was wait for the next call.

But it never came.

Shirley's house is the first on the right as you head up into the village. I've only ever walked up there a couple of times, and that was with Mum a long time ago. At that time, she was still following the advice she'd been given — by almost everyone — that the best way for me to get over my fears was to face up to them. She hated making me do it, and she soon realized that — for me — it was actually the worst thing to do, but she didn't know that then.

But although I've only *physically* walked up to Shirley's a few times, I've made the cyber-journey countless times on my laptop — studying the satellite view, zooming in and out on Google Earth, following the route step by step on street view, calculating times and distances ...

I do this for every journey Mum makes. I need to know where she is, how far away she is, and how long it'll be before she gets back.

Which is why I know that:

1) the distance between our house and Shirley's is 527 yards.

2) the average human walking speed is roughly three miles per hour.

3) so normally it would take Mum about six minutes to walk up to Shirley's.

But today wasn't a normal day.

Even if the snowplow had been through, and the worst of the snow had been cleared from the road, the conditions out there were still going to be pretty bad, and it was bound to take longer than usual for Mum to walk up to Shirley's. I doubted she'd make it in under ten minutes. It was probably going to be closer to fifteen minutes, or even longer. But as long as she kept calling me every five minutes, as long as I knew she was okay, and as long as I knew she was still on her way . . .

I wasn't too worried at first when the second five minutes had passed and she still hadn't called. *It probably doesn't mean anything,* I told myself. *She's probably just lost the signal on her phone or been distracted by something or maybe her hands are so cold now that it's taking her a bit longer to get the phone out of her pocket . . .*

I stared at the phone in my hand, willing it to ring.

A minute passed.

Two minutes . . .

Three.

Now I was worried.

Four.

More than worried.

My hand was trembling as I pressed the speed-dial key and put the phone to my ear.

The connection went straight to voice mail.

I ended the call and tried again.

It went straight to voice mail again.

"Mum?" I said after the beep. "Where are you? What's happening? Why aren't you answering your phone?"

I ended the call again and immediately called Shirley. Her cell phone went straight to voice mail too, and when I tried her landline, all I got was the empty crackle and hiss of a dead line.

I was desperate to try Mum's phone again, but I forced myself to wait. She might be trying to call me now, and if I kept calling her all the time, she'd never get through. I sent her a text — *r u ok mum? pls call me x* — and then I just sat there, staring at the phone . . .

Staring, waiting . . .

Hurting.

Another five minutes passed.

I called Mum again and left another shaky-voiced message.

One forty-five came and went, and the sickening terror just grew and grew, until at some point my physical self couldn't cope with it anymore, and it made the decision to shut me down.

I couldn't do anything then.

Couldn't move, couldn't think. Couldn't feel. All I could do was sit there in a senseless stupor, my mind in a trance, barely even conscious of reality . . .

Elliot?

Ellamay's voice was a long way away.

Elliot!

A bit louder, a bit closer.

ELL!! EE!! OTT!!

"You don't have to shout," I muttered. "I'm not deaf."

Never mind deaf, she replied. *I thought you were dead.*

It took me a while to drag myself out of the stupor, and when I did finally manage it — with a lot of help from Ella — the fear it had been hiding me from came back with a vengeance. It was as if I'd been anesthetized, unable to feel any pain, and now the anesthetic had worn off, and the pain had come back again. The pain was fear, and I could feel it stabbing into every molecule of my body.

But at least I had my self back.

It was agony, but it was me.

We need to get going, Ella said.

"I know."

I closed my eyes, picturing Shirley's house in my head, then I zoomed out and pictured the journey between our house and hers.

527 yards.

It's not far, Ella said encouragingly.

"It is if you're really small."

20

Shocked White

Jenner glanced at his watch again. It was just past one thirty, and Gordon still wasn't back.

They were in Shirley's living room. The curtains were closed, and Shirley was sitting on the floor by the radiator, bound and gagged. Her ankles were bound with baling wire, her hands similarly secured behind her back (and additionally tied to the radiator), and her mouth was gagged with a strip of duct tape. Her face was shocked white, her eyes wide with fear. Blood was oozing from a nasty-looking gash on the side of her head, the redness bright against her ashen skin. Jenner had hit her when she'd gone for his face with her fingernails, trying to claw out his eyes. He'd cracked her in the head with the barrel of his pistol — not too hard, but hard enough — and she hadn't given him any trouble after that.

"You didn't say anything about a gun," Dake had said when he'd seen the pistol.

Jenner had stared at him. "You got a problem with it?"

"No . . . it's just . . . you should have told me."

"Why?"

"Because . . . I don't know. You just should have told me, that's all."

Now Jenner was looking at his watch again. He knew he'd only just looked at it a minute ago, and he knew he was only checking it again because he was getting really edgy, and he didn't know what else to do, and he also knew that if Gordon didn't show up soon . . .

"What was that?" Dake said.

Jenner had heard it too — the sound of the front door being opened. A key turning in the lock, the door creaking faintly on its hinges . . .

"Is that him?" Dake whispered.

Jenner frowned, confused. "I didn't hear a car. Did you — ?"

"Shirley? Hello?"

It was a woman's voice, calling out from the hallway.

"Shirley? Where are you? Is everything all right?"

Jenner and Dake heard the front door being closed, then footsteps moving along the hallway toward the living room.

"Shirley? Where *are* you?"

The living room door was open, and the first thing Grace saw when she got to the doorway was a ratty little man in a cheap Santa Claus costume pointing a gun at her head.

21

THE DOOR

I'm back in the hallway now. Coat, hat, boots, gloves . . .

Cold sweat running down my back.

It's three thirty in the afternoon, Christmas Eve, and I've just taken my last remaining pill.

(Bye-bye for now, Mr. Beastie . . .

Bye-bye.)

My heart's still pounding. I'm still shaking and shivering, I still feel sick, and every cell in my body is still screaming at me to turn around and run, but thanks to the Moloxetine — or at least my psychological reaction to taking it — I don't feel quite so terrified anymore. I'm still scared to death, but I'm no longer so afraid of *being* scared to death.

The howling demon has been quieted.

For now.

But it won't stay silent for long.

I know that. I know there's no time to waste. I know I just have to do it, right now . . . just step over to the front door . . . one step . . . two steps . . .

That's it, Elliot, keep going.

. . . three steps . . . four . . .

Now open the door.

. . . the door . . .

Don't think about it. Just open it.

. . . don't think about it . . .

Open it!

The sudden sharpness of Ella's voice cuts through my fear-crazed head and spurs me into action. I reach up and take hold of the doorknob, turn it to the left, and pull, and—*BAM!!*—the door crashes open in the wind, almost yanking my arm off, and as it slams back against the wall with a juddering smash, I'm suddenly engulfed in a roaring white hell. The fury of the wind is staggering, rocking me back on my heels and almost knocking me off balance, and as the whirlwind of snow explodes all around me—driving ice-cold needles into my face—I instinctively turn away from it, covering my head with my hands and cowering against the wall.

It's no good . . .

I can't do it.

It's impossible.

No, it's not.

I can't go out there.

Yes, you can.

"No."

Glass smashes behind me as a painting is blown off the wall. A door slams somewhere, something else crashes to the floor . . .

I have to close the door.

No, Elliot.

I start backing away from the wall, hunched over against the wind, reaching out blindly for the door . . .

No.

. . . my gloved hand touches the door. I feel for the edge of it, get a good grip, then start pulling it away from the wall . . .

Don't, Elliot. Please . . .

"I'll try again in a minute. I just need to shut the door for now —"

If you don't go now, you never will.

The door won't move. The wind's too strong. I shuffle around, get both hands on the door, and pull it as hard as I can. It begins to move, and when it's far enough away from the wall, I squeeze in behind it so I can use my weight to push it shut.

Never mind, Elliot, Ella says sadly. *You did your best.*

"I haven't given up. I just told you that. I'm going to try again in a minute."

It's all right. You don't have to keep pretending for my sake. I understand why you can't do it. I know you can't help it.

The door's at the halfway point now. If I let go of it and step away, the wind's going to blow it back against the wall, but if I give it another little shove, the wind's going to get in behind it and slam it shut. And then everything will be calm and quiet again. I'll be safe from the roaring white wind. And my pounding heart will gradually slow down and stop hammering so hard against my ribs that it physically hurts . . .

And Mum will still be gone.

I lift my head, shield my eyes with my hand, and gaze out into the wildness.

She's out there somewhere, Ella says quietly.

I look up at the sky and see nothing but white darkness.

She needs you.

"Hold my hand," I whisper.

We step out through the doorway together, out into the bone-numbing cold, and when the front door slams shut behind us, there's a finality about the dull wooden *thump* that makes me think the door's never going to open again.

22

A WORLD OF GRAY-BROWN SKELETONS

The snow is thick on the ground, almost up to my knees in some places, and as I head up the path toward the front gate, with the flashlight gripped firmly in my hand, I realize that this is probably only the second or third time I've ever been out in the snow. The last time was so long ago that all I can really remember is desperately wanting to go back inside, but not being able to move because I was too scared of slipping in the snow and falling over. I've got the same sense of insecurity now — not trusting the ground beneath my feet — and I don't know how to deal with it.

I simply don't know how you're supposed to walk in the snow.

At first, I try taking big, high steps, lifting my knees right up, but that leaves me balancing on one leg for too long, and it doesn't feel very safe. So then I try walking without lifting my feet at all, shuffling along like a ski-less skier — sliding one foot forward, then the other, and the other — making my way *through* the snow rather than up and over it. And for a while, it seems to be working. It's slow going, and it's not easy — my legs are already starting to ache — but at least I feel relatively safe.

But then, just as I'm beginning to make some progress, a black snake whips up out of the snow and sinks its fangs into my leg.

I leap back in fear, clutching at the pain in my leg, and as I stagger away from the snake, my feet get caught in the snow, and I feel myself toppling over. As I hit the ground — back first and arms outstretched, like a snow angel — the black snake flops down beside me. I instinctively flinch away from it, raising my hand to protect my face, but the snake doesn't do anything, it just lies there, perfectly still, utterly lifeless . . . and when I finally find the courage to shine my flashlight at it and take a good look, it's immediately obvious that it's not a snake. Of course it's not a snake. Snakes don't slither around in the snow, do they? It's a length of black cable, that's all it is. Just a length of black cable. And when I shine my flashlight up at the house, I can see where it came from. The junction thing (the thing that joins the telephone line to the house) is half hanging off the wall, and the telephone cable itself has been ripped off in the storm. The cable must have been buried in the snow, and when

I slid my foot forward, the loose end must have sprung up out of the snow and whipped against my leg.

You've been bitten by a cable snake, Ella says, smiling.

If my teeth weren't chattering so hard, I would have smiled with her.

I'm suddenly incredibly cold, I realize. Deep down inside, I'm freezing.

And I haven't even reached the front gate yet.

The village road is just about wide enough for two cars, but it's too narrow to have a sidewalk until it broadens out a bit when it reaches the village. Both sides of the road are lined with either thick hedges (of hawthorn and hazel and holly) or drystone walls — and sometimes both — and there are big old trees growing out of the hedgerows at irregular intervals all the way up to the village. In summer and spring, the hedges and trees form a lush green arch that's so overgrown in some places that it turns the road into a tunnel, but now — in the depths of winter — the only greenery left is the strangle of ivy wrapped around tree trunks and the dark spikiness of holly. Everything else is barren and bare, like a world of gray-brown skeletons, their lifeless bones frosted with snow.

The fields that lie beyond the hedges on either side of the road are bleak and desolate too. Those on the left stretch out into the distance, eventually merging into the moors, and the fields on the right lead across to the edge of the valley and the woods down below.

The woods . . .

The woods.

They're almost too terrifying to describe.

Imagine a steep-sided valley, a great trench of densely wooded land that follows the course of a fast-flowing river from the outskirts of town all the way up to the village and beyond, and then try to picture yourself clambering down one of the treacherous trails that wind their way down the precarious slope into the dark heart of the woods. There's a silence down here, an eerie hush that magnifies the smallest sound, turning every snapped twig and rustle of leaves into something that's coming to get you. The density of the woods seems to soak up and deaden any external noises too, so although the river's nearby, the furious rush of the water sounds as if it's a long way away . . . until, that is, you break out of the woods onto the river bank, and then all of a sudden the crashing roar of the river is so ear-splittingly loud that you can't hear anything else at all.

Imagine that . . .

Imagine it.

I don't want to, but I can't help it.

My imagination of the woods and the river is just about all I've got. It's based on a real experience — a barely remembered walk along the river with Mum and Shirley when I was two or three years old . . . still in a stroller . . . before Mum knew what was wrong with me, before she knew why I cried all the time. She thought it might help to take me for a gentle wander along the river, and if you start the walk from the National Trust pathway in town, which we did, it *is* just a gentle wander. But all I could see from my stroller, and all I'd come to remember, was the vast towering darkness of the wooded slopes, looming up into the sky like the walls of hell, and a furious roar of crashing water that seemed to come from nowhere and everywhere.

I cried and howled.

Mum took me home.

And I've had nightmares about the woods ever since.

The one good thing about my encounter with the cable snake is that the back of my pants are soaking wet and freezing cold from lying in the snow, which obviously isn't good in itself, but it means that if I don't keep moving, the icy dampness seeping through to my skin is just going to get worse and worse. Moving doesn't make it that much better, but a bit better is a lot better than nothing at all.

So I get to my feet.

Brush myself down.

Take a deep breath . . .

And suck in a lungful of icy-cold air and snow.

And then, when I've finally stopped choking and coughing, I put my head down and get going.

23

BITS OF BONE AND CLICKY WET THINGS

The snow isn't too thick on the main part of road (where I'm guessing it's been plowed fairly recently), but all along the sides of the road, and up against the hedges, the snow's piled in mountainous white heaps and windblown drifts, some of which are higher than me. So I don't have any choice where to walk. I have to keep to the middle part of the road. Which makes me feel incredibly vulnerable, and far too noticeable, and belly-achingly scared.

The middle of the road is for cars.

It's their territory.

I don't belong here.

At least the cars will be going quite slowly, Ella says. *Even the dimmest monkem isn't going to drive fast in these conditions.*

"Yeah, I guess . . ."

So when you hear one coming, you'll have plenty of time to get out of the way. Especially since it's so quiet.

She's right. It *is* quiet. The wind seems to have died away now, and there's an unnatural stillness to the winter darkness, a muffled white silence that feels as if the whole world has been softened and hushed by the snow. The quiet whiteness is relatively comforting (both sound- and color-wise), but I know it's only a temporary shroud, and that underneath it lie all kinds of horrors.

There's a streetlight just across from the house. It's not dazzlingly bright, but with the lightening effect of the snow, it's enough to let me see where I'm going without the flashlight. I turn it off (to save the batteries), put it in my pocket, then set off up the road.

All I can hear is the crunch of my footsteps, the flutter of my breath, and the beating drum of my heart.

I keep going.

Head down, eyes to the ground.

One step at a time.

My shadow precedes me, a monstrous thing cast by the street-light behind me, and as I move farther away from the light, the shadow changes shape — distorting, twisting, warping — and I can't help feeling that it's mocking me, taunting me with grotesque visions of what I really am, or could be, or will be . . .

I don't like it . . .

I don't *like* it.

Something takes hold of me then, a sudden strange fury, and I lash out in mindless anger at my shadow — lunging forward and stomping on it, cursing it, kicking it, jumping on it with both feet, desperately trying to obliterate it, destroy it, kill it . . . but it's a shadow. You can't kill your own shadow. It's always going to get away from you no matter how fast you move. All you're going to end up doing is stomping around in the snow like a lunatic. And if someone happens to see you . . .

"What on earth's he doing?"

"Looks like he's stamping on something."

"Stamping on what?"

Joe and Olive Thwaite, an elderly couple from the village, were on their way to Darlington to pick up their daughter and granddaughter from the train station. It's normally a half-hour drive at most, but because of the conditions — and Joe's self-imposed speed limit of twenty miles per hour — they'd allowed themselves an extra hour for the journey.

"It's what's-his-name, isn't it?" Olive said, leaning forward to peer through the windshield. "You know, the boy from the big house . . . the one who never goes out?"

"The crazy boy?"

"Don't call him that."

"Why not? I mean, look at him . . ." Joe shook his head. "Whatever he's doing, it's not normal, is it?"

Olive couldn't argue with that.

"Do you think we should stop?" she said.

"What for?"

"To make sure he's all right."

"Does he *look* all right?"

"You know what I mean. We should at least let his mother know he's out here. We can't just —"

"He's seen us."

I would have seen the car a lot sooner if I hadn't been so intent on trying to annihilate my shadow. As it is though, because it's going so slowly that it's barely making a sound, I don't realize it's there until the twin beams of the headlights sweep over me, and my shadow suddenly goes crazy — twisting around, splitting in two, before fading out and reappearing behind me.

I look up at the approaching car, shielding my eyes from the glare of the headlights.

It's moving slowly, tires crunching quietly in the snow.

There are two old monkems in the front, a man and a woman. I can't see if anyone's in the back.

The car's getting closer . . .

A ton of growling metal . . .

Heading straight for me.

I can't think now. I'm too scared.

I can't move, can't breathe . . .

It's all right, Elliot. It's all right . . .

"I don't know what to do. What do I do?"

You need to move to the side of the road.

"I can't move."

Yes, you can. You're blocking the road. Just move over a bit and let them pass.

"I can't —"

If you don't move, they'll have to stop.

My legs don't seem to belong to me anymore. I want to move, I'm telling them to move, but they aren't responding.

Hurry up, Elliot.

The car's slowing down now, getting ready to stop . . .

Without really knowing what I'm doing, I lean over backward and slightly to the left, moving the top half of my body as far as it'll go, and then a bit farther, and a little bit farther again, forcing myself off balance, until finally, just as I'm about to fall over, my legs react and instinctively do what's necessary to keep me on my feet. And once they get going, staggering me backward (and slightly to the left) to retain my balance, all I have to do is use the momentum to steer my stumbling body over to the side of the road.

"What's he doing now?"

"Do you think he's drunk? He looks drunk."

"Maybe it's drugs."

"He doesn't look well, does he?"

"He looks dreadful."

I'm standing at the side of the road now — head down, hands in pockets, eyes to the ground — and there's plenty of room for the car to pass by. I realize the two monkems must have seen me stomping around in the middle of the road, then leaning over backward for no apparent reason, and I'm pretty sure they must think I'm insane. I hope so anyway. Because if they think I'm insane, there's a good chance they're not going to stop. You don't stop your car for a stomping lunatic, do you? You don't even make eye contact with them. It's too risky. You never know what they might do.

Unfortunately for me, though, these two monkems are either incredibly stupid or incredibly kind, because instead of just driving past, they actually slow down and pull up right next to me.

I still can't bring myself to look at them, but I know they're there. I can hear the rattly old car engine chugging away. I can smell the exhaust fumes. I can sense them both looking at me. And as I hear the driver's window sliding open, I can't help thinking that if I don't look back at them, I'll be okay . . . they'll go away . . . in fact, if I don't look at them, they won't even exist —

"Are you all right, son?"

The driver's voice. Male, gruff, a North Yorkshire accent.

I can't reply, can't raise my eyes, can't stop the desperate pleading in my head — *please go away, please go away, please go away, please go away* . . .

"Does your mother know you're out here?"

My head snaps up at the mention of Mum, and I look the old monkem in the eye. "Have you seen her?"

"Who?"

"My mum. Have you seen her?"

The old monkem-man frowns. "I don't understand . . ."

I don't like his mouth. It's kind of old and worn-out and a bit drooly, and he can't seem to close it properly — it just hangs half open all the time — and his teeth are all stained and crooked and snaggly, like they've been fixed in his gums by a blind person in a hurry . . . and when he opens his mouth wider to speak, a string of drool gets stuck between his lips, and for a few hideous moments, his mouth turns into a dark cave full of bits of bone and clicky wet things and slobbers of foul liquid oozing from the roof and the walls —

"Are you looking for your mum?"

It's a different voice, a female voice. I blink hard — once, twice—forcing the image of the cave from my mind, and when it's gone, I can see that the old monkem-lady in the passenger seat is leaning across the monkem-man and looking up at me through the open window.

"What?" I say to her.

"Are you looking for your mum?" she repeats.

"No."

I don't know why I say that. It just comes out.

Ellamay doesn't understand it either.

Tell them, she says.

"I can't."

They can help you.

"You can't what?" the monkem-lady says.

"What?"

"You said, 'I can't.'"

They're all right, Ella tells me. *They're just a nice old couple. You don't have to be scared of them.*

"He's got a cave in his face."

No, he doesn't.

"He's not right," I hear the monkem-man say quietly to the monkem-lady.

Just ask them to take you up to Shirley's, Ella says. *They won't mind.*

"I think I'd better take him back to his house," the monkem-lady says.

111

"Are you sure that's a good idea?"

"We can't just leave him out here."

"What if we take him back and no one's there? What are we going to do with him then?"

"I don't know. But if we don't take him back, we won't know if anyone's there or not, will we?" She stoops down and starts reaching under her seat for something. "Turn the engine off, Joe."

Two things happen almost simultaneously then. As the monkem called Joe reaches for the ignition, the monkem-lady finds what she's looking for under the seat and starts pulling it out. It seems to get stuck. She adjusts her grip on it, wiggles it around a bit, then pulls again. This time it comes out more easily. And when I see what it is, my heart turns to ice. It's fairly dark inside the car, and I only catch a quick glimpse of this thing the monkem-lady's pulling out, and I don't actually see all of it, so I could be mistaken . . . it might *not* be a rifle, but it's definitely a longish metal tube (like a rifle barrel), and it definitely has some kind of handle attachment near one end (like the trigger guard of a rifle), and when I hear the car engine being switched off, and I see the monkem-lady opening her door, and a split second later an ear-splitting *BANG!* rips through the air . . .

I run like a wild thing.

Blind and thoughtless and crazed with terror . . .

Heart screaming, legs pumping . . .

Staggering and stumbling through the snow . . .

And all the time I'm expecting to hear another gunshot . . . another crack of the rifle . . . and I can feel the terrible thud of the bullet hitting me in the back . . . I can physically feel it . . . it's there, right there, between my shoulder blades . . . I can *feel* it. And no matter how fast I run, I can't get away from it.

But I keep running anyway.

It's all I have.

My mind's so fogged up with fear that I'm not really aware of direction or distance, but when I hear the old monkem-lady shouting out from behind me — *HEY! HOLD ON! WHAT ARE YOU DOING? COME BACK!* — and I instinctively glance over my shoulder, I realize that I'm about thirty yards from the monkems' car, and that I'm running up the road, toward the village, rather than back to the house.

I slow down, cautiously jogging to a halt, then turn around and look back at the monkems again. As I gaze down the road, my gasping breath misting in the ice-cold air, I see the monkem-lady standing next to the car, facing me, and I'm surprised to see that instead of holding the rifle to her shoulder and aiming it at me, she seems to be leaning on it, as if it's a walking stick . . .

"DAFFY!"

The sudden shout comes from behind me, from up the road—a desperate yell that rips through the air and crashes into my heart.

"DAFFY! NO!"

I spin around, my blood racing, and I see a great black beast hurtling toward me.

24

The Crazy Wolf

"DAFFY! COME HERE! NOW!"

In the snow-white gloom, I see it all in an instant — the monstrous black dog charging down the road toward me, its leash flapping loosely from its collar . . .

"COME HERE!"

. . . its fangs bared, its wild eyes fixed on me . . .

"DAFFY!"

. . . and the monkem-lady farther up the road, chasing after the beast, shouting at the top of her voice, trying to call it back . . .

"HERE!"

. . . and the other dogs she has with her, two nasty-looking brown things, both smaller than the black one, but just as wild-looking . . . both straining on their leashes, yapping and barking and growling at me . . .

"COME HERE!"

. . . and it all explodes inside me with a blinding blast of fear that shocks me into action and sends me scrabbling frantically through the snow toward a barred metal gate on the right-hand side of the road.

The black dog's less than thirty feet away from me and closing fast, and although I'm fairly sure I can just about get to the gate before it gets to me, I can see now that the gate's locked with a padlock and chain, which means I'm going to have to climb over it, but I can also see that it's covered with wire mesh, which means there are no easy footholds, so climbing over it isn't going to be easy.

I glance over my shoulder.

The black dog's fifteen feet away now, getting bigger and wilder with every step.

"IT'S ALL RIGHT!" the monkem-dog-lady yells at me. *"HE WON'T HURT YOU!"*

The gate's about six feet tall, and as I race up to it, I know I've only got a couple of seconds before the dog gets to me, so rather than stopping and trying to clamber over the gate, I just launch myself at it, leaping as high as I can, hoping my momentum will take me over the top, and that the snow in the field on the other side will cushion my fall.

But unfortunately it doesn't work out that way.

Instead of flying over the gate, I somehow end up draped

over the top of it—my upper half hanging down on the field side, my legs dangling down on the road side. I hang there for a moment—just long enough to realize that the top bar of the gate is digging painfully into my belly, and I'm badly winded, and for some reason my left knee hurts like hell—and then the whole gate clatters violently as the great black beast crashes into it, and as it stands there on its hind legs, its front paws against the gate, barking fiercely through the fence at my upside-down face—*OWROWROW-OWROWROWROWROW!*—I reach down with both hands, grab hold of a metal bar through the wire mesh, and pull as hard as I can. I have to wriggle around quite a bit and kick out with my legs, but eventually my weight starts to shift and I feel myself tipping over the gate into the field. I'm almost there, just giving my body a final heave, when the dog leaps up and clamps its teeth into my Wellington-booted right foot. I let out a yell, and so does the monkem-dog-lady . . .

"*NO! DAFFY! LEAVE!*"

. . . but the beast takes no notice. It just keeps yanking and tugging at my foot—snarling, growling, shaking its head from side to side—and the only thing that stops me being badly bitten and dragged back over the gate is the fact that the Wellington boots are too big for me. The crazy wolf has hold of the front end of the boot, where my toes would be if the boots fit me properly, so instead of biting my foot, all the beast's got is a mouthful of rubber and scrunched-up newspaper.

It snarls viciously and yanks hard on the boot again, but this time, instead of tensing up and trying to fight back, I let my right foot go limp. The loose-fitting boot immediately slips off, taking my sock with it, and just for a moment the dog is caught by surprise — stumbling back with the boot in its mouth, not quite sure what to do — and that brief moment is all I need. By the time the dog's recovered — dismissively flinging the boot to one side and launching itself at me again — I've already heaved myself over the gate, and now I'm lying on my back in the snow on the other side.

The beast roars furiously at me through the wire-meshed gate — *OWROWROW! OWROW!* — and as I quickly get to my feet, I catch a glimpse of the monkem-dog-lady turning the corner into the gateway, red-faced and out of breath, scowling, still struggling to control the two yapping and snarling brown dogs.

"DAFFY!" she screams at the beast. *"COME HERE! RIGHT NOW!"*

The beast ignores her — *OWROWROWROWROW!*

She looks at me. "I'm *so* sorry about this . . . are you all right?"

I turn and run.

25

THE SNOW CAVE

It's not easy running through snow that in places comes up to
your knees, especially with one bare foot, but nothing matters
when you're running scared, nothing can stop you.

Nothing at all . . .

Nothing.

I'm running alongside the hedge to my left (the one that
runs parallel to the road), and as I'm leaping and bounding like
a startled deer through the snow, I'm vaguely aware of shouting
voices calling out to me from the gate — *"HEY! HOLD ON!
IT'S ALL RIGHT! COME BACK!"* I think one of the voices is
the monkem-dog-lady, and the other one sounds like the old-
monkem-lady-with-the-rifle. Part of me wants to turn around
and shout at them — *"GO AWAY! PLEASE! JUST LEAVE ME
ALONE!"* — but another part of me, the deep-down primitive
part, just wants to disappear into a hole in the ground and

lie there curled up into a ball with my eyes closed tightly and my hands clamped over my ears . . . and that desire is so over-powering that when I come to a chest-high snowdrift that's half hidden behind a massive old oak tree, there's nothing I can do to stop myself diving into it.

Nothing at all . . .

Nothing.

White nothing, cold dark white . . . I dig down into it, bury-ing myself deep in the snow . . . down into the icy silence . . . down, down, down into my hole in the ground . . . and then I just lie there, curled up into a ball, with my eyes closed tightly and my hands clamped over my ears . . .

And the outside world disappears.

It's all right now, Elliot, Ellamay says quietly after a while. *They've gone.*

"Are you sure?"

The voices stopped ten minutes ago, and about five minutes later the car started up and drove off down the road.

"What about the dog?"

It's gone. They've all gone. You're safe. You can uncover your ears and open your eyes.

I cautiously take my hands from my ears and slowly open my eyes. Silence. Just the soundless fall of the snow and the faint sigh of a low wind skimming across the field. The snow cave is dark, but not scary-dark—its pure-white walls lightening it enough to keep the black-fears at bay.

Are you okay now? Ella says.

"My foot's cold. It hurts."

Give it a good rub. You need to keep the circulation going.

I do as she says, rubbing my bare foot with both hands.

Have you got anything you can use to wrap it up?

As I search through my coat pockets, hoping to find a scarf or a woolly hat or something, I realize with a sinking heart that all the stuff that should be in my pockets is no longer there— phone, house keys, flashlight . . . all gone. They must have fallen out when I was throwing myself over the gate.

Check your pants pockets, Ellamay says.

I shake my head. "I never put anything in my pants pockets."

Why not?

"I don't know . . . I just don't."

Check them anyway.

I know they're empty, but there's no point in arguing about it, so I quickly search through them, front and back.

"Nothing," I say.

Ellamay sighs.

I wouldn't blame her if she was annoyed or exasperated with me. If I'd put all my stuff in my pants pockets, I probably wouldn't have lost it. But I know Ella isn't annoyed with me. She never is. She understands . . . she always understands.

She knows I don't have much practical pocket experience—if you barely ever leave the house, you don't need to know much about pockets—and as we both lapse into a snowbound silence, we're as together as we always are.

Together.

As one.

And here in the sanctuary of our snow cave we feel as safely cocooned as we've ever been—curled up together, keeping each other warm, our hearts beating as one . . .

It becomes us.

It is us.

It was us.

Before it all went wrong.

"Maybe we could just stay here this time," I whisper.

Ella doesn't answer for a while, and I can hear the depth of sorrow in her silence.

"Sorry, Ella . . . I didn't mean to—"

It's okay, she mutters. *I just . . . I don't know . . . it just got to me for a moment, that's all.*

"Can you remember it?" I ask hesitantly.

Dying?

"Yeah."

I'm not sure. I remember something. I remember being alive, with you, inside Mum, but after that . . . there's nothing . . . less than nothing . . . no darkness, no light . . . no time, no where or when . . . no nothing, forever and ever and ever and ever . . .

"It was terrifying," we say together, our eyes filling with tears. It still is.

We sink back into our silence again, and for a while we just sit there together, gazing around the snow cave, remembering, imagining, wondering what might have been . . .

Eventually Ella sighs again and says, *We can't stay here, Elliot. We have to get going.*

I nod reluctantly and glance at my watch.

What time is it, Cinders?

"What?"

Ella smiles, glancing at my bare right foot. *Cinderella lost her glass slipper, you've lost your Wellington boot. If you don't get home by midnight, you'll turn into a pumpkin.*

"No," I say, shaking my head, "you've got it all wrong. It's Cinderella's golden carriage that turns into a pumpkin, not her. And she gets home before midnight anyway."

No, she doesn't.

"She does."

She doesn't.

"She does."

All right. But even if she does —

"What was that?"

What?

"That noise."

What noise?

"Listen."

We listen together to the silence, and after a while I begin to wonder if I was mistaken. Maybe I didn't hear anything after all. Maybe it was just in my mind, or just something blowing in the wind, or maybe it was—

KAH!

It's much louder now.

What the hell is it? Ella says.

KAH!

"I don't know," I mumble, cowering back against the cave wall. "But whatever it is, it's getting closer."

26

A Fluorescent Bird of Paradise

"What are we going to do?" Dake asked Jenner. "I mean, we can't just keep waiting for him, can we?"

"Do you want to give up?"

"Well, no, but —"

"If you want to go, just go. I'm not stopping you."

"I never said anything about going, did I? I was just wondering what we're going to do if he doesn't show up, that's all."

"He'll show up."

Jenner glanced over at Shirley and Grace. They were both sitting on the floor by the radiator now, both bound and gagged, and both looking the worse for wear. Shirley's complexion was a sickly gray-white, and although the gash on the side of her head had stopped bleeding, it was badly bruised and swollen. Grace had a nasty-looking wound on her face too. She'd fought like a wild thing when the two men had grabbed her — screaming at them, kicking and punching, biting and scratching — and Jenner had had to hit her twice, and hit her hard, to knock the fight out of her. His first blow, a vicious punch, had cracked her jaw and loosened one of her teeth, and the second — a brutal hammering with the butt of his pistol — had caught her just below her right eye. The eye was already blackening, and it had swollen up so much that she couldn't see out of it anymore.

She watched, one-eyed, as Jenner came over and stood in front of them. He gazed coldly at them, idly scratching at his increasingly itchy Santa beard with the barrel of the pistol, and then — without looking around — he said to Dake, "Are the cell phones still out?"

Dake reached into his pocket and pulled out three cell phones — one of them was his, the other two were Shirley's and Grace's. He looked at them one by one, checking the signal indicators, but nothing had changed since the last time he'd checked. No bars, no reception.

"Nope, nothing," he told Jenner. "It must be the weather."

"Check the landline again."

Dake went over to a small table by the settee and picked up a handset. He pressed the call button, put the phone to his ear, then shook his head.

"It's still out," he said.

Jenner just stood there for a while, calmly thinking things

through, then he casually raised his pistol, leveled it at Grace's head, and turned to Shirley.

"Same rules as before," he told her. "I'm going to take the tape off your mouth and ask you some questions. If you lie to me, or scream for help, I'll put a bullet in her head. Understand?"

Shirley nodded.

Jenner had already questioned her about Gordon — what time did she expect him back? why was he so late? where could he have gone? — and when Shirley had told him that her son was due back at one o'clock, and that she had no idea why he wasn't home yet, or where he might be, Jenner knew she was telling the truth. He was a consummate liar himself, and he'd always prided himself on his ability to recognize a lie when he heard one, and he was as sure as he could be that Shirley wasn't lying.

When he stooped down this time to peel the tape from her mouth, she couldn't help flinching away from him, but he didn't make anything of it. He just reached out, grabbed an edge of the tape, and quickly ripped it from her mouth. She squeezed her eyes shut and grimaced at the pain, but she didn't cry out.

"All right?" Jenner grunted.

She nodded.

"So what do you think?" he said. "What's happened to Gordon?"

"I really don't know."

"What would he have done if his car wouldn't start or if he got stuck in the snow somewhere?"

"He would have tried calling me."

"And if he couldn't get through?"

"He would have walked back."

"Really?"

"I know my son."

"I'm sure you do. How long do you think it would take him to walk here?"

"From where? The bank?"

"Yeah."

Shirley thought about it. "Forty-five minutes, maybe. Something like that."

"So if he'd started walking at around twelve thirty, he would have been back by now, wouldn't he?"

Shirley nodded. "He would have been back ages ago."

"And if his car got stuck in the snow somewhere between town and here, and he'd left it and started walking, he would have been back even sooner, wouldn't he?"

"Yes."

"So we can rule out car trouble."

"I guess so."

"Maybe he's dead," Dake suddenly piped up.

There was a stunned pause for a moment, then all three of them gazed over at him.

"What?" he said, bewildered by the looks on their faces. "It would explain everything, wouldn't it? I mean, he can hardly walk home if he's dead, can he?"

Gordon wasn't dead. Far from it. In fact, at that very moment — 4:34 p.m. — he'd never felt more alive. Admittedly, he'd never felt quite so strange either, and as he approached his silver Vauxhall Corsa and beeped the lock, he was amazed to see the sound of the beep turning into a fluorescent bird of paradise and flying up into the snowy night sky.

"Sheesh," he muttered.

The echoes of his voice swirled all around him, a hundred thousand tiny "sheeshes" whirling and spiraling together, like a vast school of silvery fish feeding on the falling snowflakes.

Gordon held out his hand. A snowflake landed on it, and he brought his hand up close to his eyes and stared at the delicate white crystal.

A memory came to him.

A voice?

No, not quite . . . just words.

. . . millions of snowflakes dropping down from the sky like invaders from another planet, silent and serene, menacing . . . awesome . . . an *alien world . . . crystals . . . symmetrical patterns . . . snow . . . snow-ball . . . snowdrop . . . drop of snow . . .*

"Snow goose," Gordon muttered, smiling to himself, "that's no goose, that's my wife . . ."

He paused, frowning, momentarily unaware of where he was, or where he'd been, or what he was doing . . . and then he blinked once, and something clicked inside his head, and although he still wasn't sure where he'd been, or why it was dark, he at least knew where he was, and what day it was.

It was Christmas Eve.

He was standing by his car, in the staff parking lot at the back of the bank, and it was time to go home.

He opened the car door and got in. As he closed the door and settled into the seat, he realized right away that something didn't feel right. He couldn't pin it down at first — it just felt different — and for a moment or two he actually wondered if he was somehow in the wrong car, but after a quick look around, he knew that wasn't it. The pine air freshener dangling from the rearview mirror was his, as was the satnav and the beaded seat cover . . . yes, this was definitely his car. There was just something . . . something missing . . . and then it struck him.

The steering wheel.

It wasn't there.

He reached out in front of him, moving his hands around

the space where the steering wheel should have been — as if, perhaps, it *was* still there, but had somehow become invisible — but he couldn't feel anything. The steering wheel simply wasn't there. The only thing he could think of was that it must have been stolen. Someone must have broken into the car and stolen his steering wheel . . .

But even as he tried to get angry about it — which he didn't really want to, but felt that he should — the truth of the matter suddenly dawned on him. He slowly turned to his right . . .

And there it was — the steering wheel. It wasn't missing. No one had stolen it. It was exactly where it should be — right in front of the driver's seat.

It was Gordon who wasn't where he should be.

He was in the wrong side of the car.

He was sitting in the passenger seat.

He started laughing then. It was just a quiet chuckle at first, but the more he thought about what he'd done, and what he'd thought — a steering-wheel thief? — the more ludicrously hysterical it all seemed, and his quiet chuckle quickly became a manic chortling, which in turn grew into a howling fit of unstoppable laughter that had Gordon doubled over in his seat, clutching tightly at the pain in his sides, while a torrent of tears streamed from his eyes.

27

THE GUINEA PIG

"Do you think he'll be all right?"

The music in the King's Head was so loud — Slade's "Merry Xmas Everybody" booming out from the speakers for at least the hundredth time — that Kaylee had to shout in Jo Dean's ear to make herself heard, and even then, her friend couldn't quite hear what she was saying.

"*WHAT?*" Jo yelled back, cupping her hand to her ear.

"*GORDON!*" Kaylee bellowed. "*DO YOU THINK HE'LL BE ALL RIGHT?*"

She'd thoroughly enjoyed every minute of Gordon's intoxicated presence over the last few hours, and when he'd left ten minutes ago, she'd laughed along with everyone else at the sight of him heading for the exit, grinning madly as he looked over his shoulder and waved good-bye. And when he'd walked smack-dab into the door, she'd almost wet herself with laughter. But at the same time, she couldn't stop worrying about the assurance she'd given Carl Jenner that Gordon would be home by one o'clock at the latest.

It was 4:35 now.

Carl wasn't going to be happy at all.

And when Carl wasn't happy . . .

Kaylee didn't want to think about that.

She'd tried calling and texting him to let him know that Gordon was going to be late, but she couldn't get a signal, and when she'd asked to borrow Jo's phone, Jo had told her that she didn't have a signal either.

There was a lull in the music now, and this time, when Kaylee repeated her question—"Do you think he'll be all right?"—Jo actually heard her.

"Who?"

"Gordon."

"Yeah," Jo said, her voice slurred, "he'll be fine." She grinned drunkenly. "Don't worry about it. He won't remember a thing."

"What did you actually put in his drink?"

Jo picked up her almost-full glass of vodka and Coke and downed it in one go. "Tell you the truth," she said, stifling a burp, "I'm not exactly sure what it was. Some kind of pill . . . you know, like a capsule? I got them off this guy I know. He said they were new, really good stuff, really potent, like a mixture of roofies, ecstasy, and acid." She grinned again. "I just opened up a couple of capsules and emptied the powder into Gordon's lager and lime."

"Have you taken them?"

Jo shook her head. "I thought I'd try them on Gordon first . . ." She let out a snort of laughter. "Gordon the guinea pig."

"What do you think —?"

"I need to pee," Jo said, getting to her feet. She swayed, her upper body circling, and she had to put her hand on the table to steady herself.

"Are you all right?" Kaylee asked her.

"Yeah, yeah . . . no problem . . ." She grinned again. "Back in a minute . . . don't go away."

As she headed for the door that led to the women's room, doing her best to walk in a straight line, the music started up again. It was Slade again, for the one hundred and first time. And for the one hundred and first time, everyone drunkenly sang along.

28

THIRTY-FIVE HEADS
(AND SEVENTY EVIL EYES)

KAH!

It's the cough of the Devil.

And ten seconds later, when its horned head appears at the entrance to the snow cave, and it stares at me with its demonic yellow eyes, I honestly think this is it — this is the end . . . I'm literally dying of fright. But then, to my amazement, the demon suddenly freezes, a look of surprise in its eyes — as if it's only just realized what it's looking at — and a moment later it rears back in fear, throwing its head to one side, and then it's gone. I can hear it running away, a panicked barreling through the snow . . . and I don't get it, I don't understand why the Devil is scared of me . . .

It's the Devil.

And I'm me.

The fear's only supposed to go one way.

It doesn't make sense.

KAH!

Unless . . .

BAAHH . . .

Unless.

It's a sheep, Elliot. That's all. It's just a sheep.

I remember now . . . the sound of a sheep coughing, like a sick old man. I remember hearing it at night sometimes, before I had my fear-proofed room.

KAH!

I remember.

I remember imagining a field full of sick old men, out there in the darkness, coughing themselves to death . . .

And I remember making myself forget it.

Come on, Elliot, Ella says. *We need to get going.*

I know she's right, but the trouble is, although sheep are nowhere near as scary as the Devil, that doesn't mean I'm not afraid of them. They're animals, they've got teeth, hooves, horns . . .

They're more afraid of you than you are of them.

"Frightened animals are dangerous."

You're an animal, aren't you? You're frightened.

It's a good point, and as I start crawling out of the snow cave — aware now that my bare foot is completely numb — I try to convince myself that I *am* a dangerous animal, and that from now on, nothing's going to get in my way, nothing's going to stop me, and if anything or anyone tries to . . .

"Oh, no . . ."

I'm kneeling at the edge of the snow cave now, and as I look across the field toward the gate, all I can see is sheep — hundreds of them, all flocked together in front of the gate, all of them facing me, all of them staring demonically at me.

You're dangerous, remember? Ellamay says. *Nothing's going to get in your way.*

"Well, yeah . . . but I didn't know there were going to be hundreds of them, did I?"

There aren't hundreds of them, Elliot. There's about thirty, thirty-five at the very most.

"That's still quite a lot."

They're sheep. They're not going to stop you getting to the gate. As soon as they see you walking toward them, they'll run away.

"But what if they don't? What if they decide to attack me instead?"

They won't.

"But what if they do?"

They won't, Elliot.

For the next thirty seconds or so, I just kneel there in the snow-whitened gloom, studying the almost motionless sheep. The faded light from the streetlamp down the road gives them an oddly unnatural look—kind of dull green and gray-ish, like the images on a CCTV monitor. A car goes down the road then, and as it passes the gate—with a brief sweep of headlights—all the sheep turn their heads to watch it. They all move at exactly the same time and in exactly the same manner. It's as if the flock itself is a single organism, with a collective consciousness of its own.

And the problem for me now is that it looks as if that con-sciousness has decided that the best thing to do at the moment is stay exactly where it is, right in front of the gate.

You have to get out of here, Ella reminds me. *Get back to the road, find your Wellington boot, get moving again.*

I stand up, take a quick look over my shoulder—just in case anything's creeping up behind me—then I start making my way through the snow toward the flock of sheep.

They don't move at all, they just carry on standing there, watching me as I limp toward them. The closer I get—and the longer they don't move—the scarier they become. I can see the wicked black slits in their eyes, and their vicious black hooves pawing at the snow. I can see the raw strength in their bodies . . .

Keep going, Elliot . . . they're going to move.

"They're not."

They are. Just keep going.

It's getting harder with every step. It's as if there's an

invisible force field between me and the sheep — a force field of fear — and the closer I get to the sheep, the stronger the force field becomes.

I'm about ten yards away from them now.

And that's it. That's as close as I can get. The force field is an invisible wall. It's physically impossible to get past it.

Keep going . . .

"I can't."

Yes, you can. Just another couple of steps.

The sheep are all tensed up and twitchy, and I know that if I move any closer, they're going to charge at me. I just know it. I can feel it.

Can you see your stuff anywhere? Ella says. *The stuff that fell out of your pockets?*

I focus on the area just in front of the gate, searching for any sign of my phone, keys, and flashlight. But it's hopeless. I can barely even see the ground because of all the sheep, and the patches that I can see are just a sheep-trampled mess of churned-up mud and snow. There's no sign of my Wellington boot either, and I wonder briefly what's happened to it. Has the monkem-dog-lady taken it with her? Maybe the two monkems in the car told her where I live, and she's left the boot at my front gate . . . ?

It doesn't matter.

Whatever's happened to it, the boot's not there anymore.

Try moving sideways, Elliot, Ella says. *See if that works.*

I take a step to my left.

Thirty-five heads (and seventy evil eyes) follow my movement. But the flock doesn't move.

I take another step to my left.

This time the sheep do react, but instead of moving away from the gate, they actually seem to relax a bit, as if they're *more* content to stay where they are. And I realize then that although I'm moving sideways, I'm actually moving away from the sheep, which serves no purpose at all.

I move back to my original position. The flock tenses up. I take two steps to my right, and the flock relaxes again.

They're not going to move.

They might if I got closer to them, but I can't. And I can't get to the gate without getting closer to them.

"I don't know what to do, Ella."

There's no reply.

"Ella?"

She's gone.

It happens sometimes. She'll be with me, talking to me, and then — for no apparent reason — she suddenly disappears. I don't know where she goes. And neither does she. *I just kind of stop being,* she told me once. *I don't have any awareness of anything. I'm just there, and then I'm not. And then I come back again.*

*

I'm so cold. And tired. The bone-deep pain in my bare foot is creeping up into my leg, and my foot feels black and rotten. Like a dead thing.

I need to rest.

I need to lie down and go to sleep . . .

But I can't.

I need to get out of here.

I start moving back from the sheep, and when I can't feel the force field at all anymore, I stop and gaze around, searching for another way out. On this side of the field, the side next to the road, there's enough light from the streetlamps to see that there aren't any other gates, and that the hawthorn hedges surrounding the field look impenetrable. They're about six feet high, and so thick and densely packed—and the thorns so razor sharp—that if I tried squeezing through, I'd be cut to pieces in seconds. And even if I could find a gap somewhere, I can see now that on the other side of the hedge there's a three-foot-high wire-mesh fence, topped with double strands of barbed wire, and on this side of the hedge there's a fairly deep ditch, which effectively makes the hedge and the fence even higher. The rest of the field is too dark to see if the fence and the ditch go all the way around, and I know that beyond that darkness at the top of the field, there's another darkness, deeper and blacker . . . the nightmare darkness of the woods.

I don't want to go there.

I can't . . .

I'd rather be cut to pieces.

I head off back the way I came, following my tracks in the snow.

There has to be another way out of here . . . there *has* to be. And if the only way to find it is by walking all the way around the field, checking every inch of the perimeter, then that's what I'll have to do.

I look at my watch.

It's 4:45.

Under normal circumstances, my last fear pill shouldn't be wearing off just yet, but these are far from normal circumstances, and I've got a terrible feeling that Mr. Beastie will soon start rattling his cage. And if that happens before I find Mum and get my pills . . . ?

No.

It can't happen.

It can't.

I'll dig myself out of here with my bare hands if I have to.

29

THE STRANGE BOY FROM THE BIG HOUSE

The four men (and a dog) were walking back to the village after a Christmas drink in the Holly Tree Inn when the Thwaites' car pulled up beside them. One of the men — Davey Price — was the Thwaites' next-door neighbor, and the other three were all from the village too, so they knew Joe and Olive fairly well. The men were about halfway between the pub and the village when the car stopped, and because there were no streetlights here, and no sidewalks either, they were all carrying flashlights.

Olive quickly told them about the strange boy from the big house who'd run off into the field, and when she'd finished telling them what had happened, she asked them if they wouldn't mind keeping an eye out for him.

"I went to the house," she explained, "but there was no one there, and we've been trying to call the police but neither of us can get a signal."

"Do you think he's in some kind of trouble?" Davey Price asked, leaning down to the open window.

Olive could smell the alcohol on his breath, but although it was quite strong—and she guessed they'd all had quite a few drinks—she could tell that Davey wasn't drunk. A bit tipsy maybe, but not drunk.

"I'm just worried about him being out on his own in this weather," Olive told Davey. "I don't think he's used to being out of his house at all, let alone in a blizzard, and if he's still out there somewhere, wandering around on his own in the darkness . . ." She shook her head. "I would have gone after him myself, but with my hip the way it is . . ."

"Did the woman with the dogs go after him?" Davey asked.

"She was going to . . . I think she felt really bad about her dog scaring him so much. But then I pointed out that if she went after him with her dogs, it'd just scare him even more."

"So what did she do?"

"She said she was going to take her dogs home and then come back out again and look for him on her own."

"Do you know her?"

"I've seen her around. She lives in one of the new houses at the top of the village. But I don't know her name."

"What about the boy? Do you know his name?"

Olive shook her head.

"I think it's Elton," the man standing beside Davey said.

Davey turned to him. "What?"

"The kid's name . . . I think it's Elton. Or Ellis. Something like that anyway. Maybe Elmer."

"Elmer?"

The man shrugged.

Davey frowned at him, then turned back to the car. He lowered his head and looked over at Joe in the driver's seat, who so far hadn't said a word.

"What do you think, Joe?" Davey asked him.

"I think if we don't get going right now," Joe said grumpily, "we're not going to get to the station in time to meet our daughter and granddaughter off the train." He looked at Olive. "That's what I think."

Davey smiled. *Same old Joe,* he thought, *as cheerful as ever.*

He turned back to Olive. "We'll find the boy, don't worry. You go and get your daughter."

30

Everything's a Monster

The field is rectangular. The shorter sides back onto the road at one end, and the woods at the other, and both the longer sides are flanked by more fields. There's definitely no way through the hedge/fence that runs parallel to the road, and when I get to the end of it and turn right, and start following the longer hedge/fence that leads away from the road and up toward the top of the field (the side that backs onto the woods), it soon becomes apparent that this hedge/fence is just as impassable as the shorter one. It has the same solid thickness of hawthorn, the same three-foot-high wire-mesh fence, and the same deep ditch at its base. And the added problems with this side of the field are that 1) the farther it gets away from the road, the less light it gets from the streetlamps, which means that by the time I've gone about twenty yards, it's so dark I can barely see where I'm going. And 2) even if I do somehow manage to find a way through the hedge/fence, there's no knowing what awaits me in the field on the other side. It could be just as inescapable as this one. Or just as sheep-infested. Or, even worse, it could have horses in it . . .

Horses.

I can picture them now in the gloom . . . grayed visions in the blackness . . . great long heads, like giant hammers . . . huge chomping teeth . . . venomous eyes . . .

A sudden burst of noise comes from the hedge/fence, the sound of rapid movement, and the shock of it hits me so hard that I stagger backward, with my hands raised to my head (to protect myself from the hedge-crashing horse), and as my booted foot slips on something, I lose my balance and fall over into the snow.

There's another brief eruption of noise, but this time it's more of a panicked rustling than a burst, and then whatever it is (and I know now that it's too small to be a hedge-crashing horse), it scurries off across the field on the other side of the hedge.

As I lie there on my back, my heart hammering in my chest, Ellamay comes back to me.

It was just a rabbit or a badger or something, she says. *Maybe a fox.* She smiles. *Whatever it was though, it wasn't a monster.*

"A fox is a monster if you're a mouse," I tell her.

Well, yeah —

"And a mouse is a monster if you're a tiny insect, and a tiny insect is a monster if you're an even tinier insect. Everything's a monster to something."

Silence.

"Ella?"

She's gone again.

As I carry on lying there, gazing up into the infinite blackness, I can't help wondering if Ella's up there somewhere . . . up among the stars, a thousand million miles away . . . or maybe she's *beyond* the stars, beyond everything . . . in a place with no life, no darkness, no light . . . no time, no where or when, no nothing, forever and ever and ever and ever . . .

No . . .

I can't think about that.

I grab a handful of snow and rub it into my face, and the ice-cold shock does the trick — dismissing the dark thoughts from my mind and bringing me back to reality.

I sit up and look around. It isn't snowing anymore. The wind's died away too. The ice-cold air is still and quiet, and a pale slice of moon is showing through the clouds.

I get to my feet, brush myself down, and get going again.

31

HALF A HUMAN LEG

The field seems to go on forever, and although the all-round whiteness prevents the darkness from being absolute, I still can't see anything with any real clarity. The seemingly endless hedge/fence is just a blurred presence, a long dark shape to the left of me, its darkness a slightly different shade to the darkness surrounding it, and while I'm still keeping my eyes on it all the time, searching hard for any sign of a gap, I honestly don't know if I'd see one if it was there.

But what else can I do apart from keep going?

There's no point in turning back, and the only other option is to simply give up—dig myself another snow cave, curl up inside it, close my eyes, and go to sleep.

I might never wake up . . .

Would that be so bad?

Yes, it would, says Ellamay.

"We'd be together again," I tell her.

We're together now.

"Not all the time."

What makes you think I want to be with you all the time?

I smile at her.

She smiles back. *Just keep going, okay?*

"Okay."

There's a weird kind of lightness at the top end of the field. It's only faint, but it seems to run all the way along the fence that separates the field from the wooded valley on the other side, and what makes it even stranger is that the valley is so utterly dark, so dense and black, that it's almost beyond darkness. It's like a vast black hole, sucking everything into its depths, devouring every little flicker of light . . . and I wonder if that's why there's a lightness to this side of the fence. The light feels safe here, the black hole can't reach it . . . or maybe it just appears lighter here in comparison to the ultra-black void of the valley.

There's no hedge or ditch on this side of the field, just the barbed-wire-topped fence, and as I hobble along through the snow — my right leg is numb from the knee down now — I'm reasonably sure that without the added barriers of the hedge and the ditch, the fence wouldn't be too difficult to climb over. There's a narrow dirt path on the other side of it. It's hidden beneath the snow now, but I know it's there because

I've seen it on Google Earth. It runs all the way along the top of the valley—with perilously steep paths leading off it that wind their way down into the dark heart of the woods—and eventually it comes out into the fields at the back of the houses in the village.

I pause for a moment, closing my eyes and picturing Shirley's house—the small yard at the back, the ramshackle fence, and beyond that the fields . . .

If only the woods weren't so paralyzingly terrifying . . .

If only.

I open my eyes.

I wouldn't even have to climb over the fence. There's a stile . . . right there in front of me. A wooden stile set into the fence. All I'd have to do is step up onto it, step across, and step down, and I'd be on the dirt path on the other side . . . the path that leads along to the field at the back of Shirley's house.

If only . . .

Why don't you just try it? Ellamay says. *You can always turn back again if it really is too scary.*

"No."

It might not be as bad as you think.

"It is. I *know* it is. And so do you. You've been there with me in the nightmares, haven't you?"

Well, yes, but they're nightmares. This is reality.

"You think there's a difference?"

She goes quiet, and I wonder for a moment if she's leaving me again, but when I can still feel her presence after a minute or two, I know she's not going anywhere just yet. She's just being quiet.

I move on, leaving the stile behind, and I start heading over to the right-hand side of the field, the final side of the rectangle.

Whatever little hope I had of finding a way out is all but gone now. I'm pretty much just going through the motions — struggling along through the snow, peering into the gloom, looking for gaps in the hedge/fence, gaps that almost certainly aren't there . . .

And then I see the lights.

At first I only see them from the corner of my eye — a flash of bright lights down at the bottom of the field — and for a second I assume they're just the headlights of a passing car, but when they don't go away, and I stop looking at the hedge/ fence and focus instead on the gate at the bottom of the field, it's obvious that the lights aren't headlights. They're flashlights, down at the gate, and there's at least four of them, which means there's at least four monkems down there.

It's too dark — and the monkems are too far away — to see clearly, but as the powerful flashlight beams keep sweeping around, I catch momentary glimpses of illuminated faces and figures, and I'm pretty sure they're all men — big coats, hats, boots. Big voices. The still air carries the murmur of their voices up the field, and although I can't make out what they're saying, there's a hardness to the voices that gives me a really bad feeling. I'm not sure why, but there's something of the hunter about them.

I hear a metallic creaking then, and as one of the monkems directs his flashlight at the gate, I see another one — a big rough-looking man with a black beard — clambering over into the field. The sheep are still there, but they've moved back from the gate now, and when the bearded monkem turns around and shines his flashlight at them, they all suddenly take off, running away into the darkness on the left-hand side of the field.

The fear's flooding through me now, emptying my stomach and chilling me to the bone, and the next sound I hear makes me feel even worse. It comes from the gate, a short sharp bark, and as my breath freezes in my throat, and I stare wide-eyed down the field, I see that three of the monkems are in the field now, and the fourth one — who's still on the other side of the gate — is bending down to pick up a dog. It's a big hefty-looking thing, and the monkem has to cradle it in both arms to lift it up. The dog barks again, and the monkem passes it over the gate to one of the others. He then climbs over the gate himself, takes the dog's leash from the other one, and squats down beside it. As the bearded monkem shines his flashlight on them, I can see the fourth one holding something out to the dog, letting it smell it. For a moment or two, I can't work out what it is.

It looks like the lower half of a human leg, including the foot, but it seems kind of floppy too, which doesn't make sense. Why would a human leg be floppy? And for that matter, why would these monkems have half a human leg in the first place, and why would they be encouraging their dog to smell it? But then one of the other monkems directs his flashlight at the monkem with the leg and the dog, and because the change of angle gives me a better view, I can see now that it's not half a leg — of *course* it's not — it's my Wellington boot. They must have found it on the other side of the gate, and they're letting the dog get my scent from it, and then the dog's going to follow my trail around the field and lead the monkems to me.

They're going to hunt me down . . .

You haven't done anything wrong, Elliot, Ella starts to say. *There's no reason for them to —*

"THERE HE IS!"

The guttural shout comes from one of the monkems. I can't see which one because all of a sudden I'm blinded by the dazzling light of a flashlight, and as I raise my hand to shield my eyes, another beam lights me up, and then the dog starts yapping and more voices ring out.

"HEY, YOU UP THERE!"

YAP-YAP-YAP-YAP-YAP . . .

"HEY, KID!"

YAP-YAP-YAP . . .

"DON'T MOVE! JUST STAY WHERE YOU ARE!"

As I run off up the field, back the way I came, I'm remotely aware that the shouts are getting louder and more desperate, but I'm not really conscious of them. I'm not conscious of anything now. I'm in automatic fear mode. My body's taken over, and all it cares about is running, getting me away from the danger. It's making me race through the snow as fast as possible, making me ignore the awful pain in my frozen foot, and at the same time it's assessing all the options and making split-second decisions. Is it best to keep going in a straightish line, following my tracks in the snow — for easier and quicker running — or is it better to start zigzagging, darting from side to side, to make it harder for the monkems to keep me in their flashlight beams? An instant later my body lunges to the right, out of the lights and into the untrammeled snow, and before the monkems have time to redirect their flashlights, it veers to the right again, and then immediately to the left. And then, as someone shouts, *"WHERE'S HE GONE?"* my bare foot hits a snow-buried rock, and I scream out in agony and tumble over into the snow.

The pain's so bad I have to grit my teeth and clamp my hand over my mouth to stop myself crying out, and as I lie there in the snow — with the flashlight beams sweeping around — I can feel the cold stickiness of blood oozing between my toes, and although it's too dark to see the gut-wrenching redness, it's still terrifying enough to sicken me to the stomach. I roll over onto my side and vomit into the snow. My stomach's empty . . . all that comes up is some yellowy goo. I spit it out, retch again, spit again, and when I feel the nausea subsiding, I rinse out my mouth with a handful of snow, and use another handful to clean up my face.

My foot hurts *so* much . . .

"ANYONE SEE WHERE HE WENT?"

"OVER THERE."

"WHERE?"

The voices are getting closer.

I can't stay here. I have to get going again.

But where?

I roll over onto my front, prop myself up on my elbows, and cautiously raise my head just enough to see over the parapet of snow. The fence at the top of the field is about ten yards away, and I'm about a third of the way across the field. I glance over my shoulder. The monkems are directly behind me, and they're a lot closer than I thought. Forty yards . . . maybe less. The flashlight beams are still searching for me, sweeping around all over the field, so at least the monkems don't know where I am yet. But if I stay here, and they keep coming this way . . .

An idea suddenly comes to me.

A way out.

There *is* a way out.

I sit up, crouch down low, and peer down the field toward the gate. The sheep haven't come back. The gate's unguarded. If I can get to it without being spotted . . .

The flashlight beams are still sweeping around the field, like searchlights hunting for an escaped prisoner. I watch them closely, waiting for the moment when none of them are shining in my direction, and then I make my move.

My mashed-up toe screams out in pain as I jump to my feet and start running, and I almost give up there and then. I can't do it . . . it hurts too much . . . I'm going to have to stop . . .

But then more shouts ring out . . .

"THERE HE GOES!"

"WHERE?"

"THERE!"

. . . and the dog starts barking . . .

YAP-YAP-YAP-YAP . . .

. . . and someone yells out, *"NO! MOLLY! NO! COME HERE!"*

. . . and a searchlight picks me out . . .

"I'VE GOT HIM!"

. . . and all this triggers a renewed flood of fear that surges through me like an electric shock, and now I couldn't stop running even if I wanted to . . . it's all I *can* do . . . and the pain can't stop me . . . it's just pain . . . a thing, a feeling . . .

YAP-YAP-YAP-YAP . . .

"MOLLY!"

I'm almost halfway across the width of the field now, running parallel to the fence at the top, and about five yards away from it. Although the monkems have me in their sights, there's still a chance I can make it to the gate before them. They're just about level with me now, around twenty yards behind me. If I feint to the right and make a sudden turn to my left, it might just surprise them enough to make them lose sight of me — at least for a few moments — and then if I run straight down the field, as fast as I can, I might just have enough of a head start to reach the gate before them.

YAP-YAP-YAP-YAP . . .

"MOLLY! HERE!"

I suddenly realize that not only has Molly the dog been barking nonstop for the last minute or so — and that one of the monkems has been yelling at her nonstop — but also that the continuous yap-yap-yapping isn't coming from behind me, where the monkems are. It started there, then began moving around the field, and right now . . .

YAP-YAP-YAP-YAP . . .

. . . it's coming from the darkness directly in front of me . . .

YAP-YAP-YAP-YAP . . .

. . . moving toward me . . .

YAP-YAP-YAP-YAP . . .

. . . and there's another sound with it . . . a muffled rumbling . . . getting closer and closer . . . louder and louder . . .

And then I see them, looming out of the darkness, stampeding through the snow, heading straight for me . . . the flock of
terrified sheep. Molly the dog's right behind them, yap-yapping
and nipping at their heels, and they're running like crazy things,
desperate to get away from her. They're not going to stop for me
in the state they're in, they're not even going to try to avoid me.
They're blind with fear, just mindless running machines, and
at the speed they're going — which is unbelievably fast — I've
only got a fraction of a second to decide what to do. If I don't do
anything, I'm going to be trampled into the ground by thirty-
odd stampeding sheep, and they're far too fast for me to outrun
them, especially as I've only got one good leg.

As I rapidly glance around, looking for an escape route, I
see three of the monkems fifteen yards behind me, and the
fourth one about the same distance away, but just over to my
left. He's marching across the field with the dog leash in his
hand and an angry scowl on his face, so I assume he's Molly's
owner.

Now one of the other three shouts out to him, *"WAIT
THERE, GEOFF! DON'T LET HIM GET PAST YOU!"* And as he
stops and turns to face me, I realize that I'm boxed in. Sheep in
front of me — almost on top of me — three monkems behind
me, and one to my left. I look despairingly to my right, knowing
what I'm going to see, and knowing I'm not going to like it.

The wooden stile.

It's right there, almost level with me, less than five yards away.

No, I can't . . .

You have to.

No.

You don't have a choice.

There's no time to think. The sheep are thundering toward me — ten yards away, nine, eight . . .

Go, Elliot!

. . . seven . . .

I can't . . .

Go!

. . . six . . .

GO!

I fling myself across to the stile, and I only just manage to scramble onto it before the rampaging sheep go crashing past. And even then, they're so closely bunched together, and so desperate, that some of them don't swerve around the wooden step of the stile, they either just smash into it and keep going, or leap right over it. And it's one of the leaping sheep's horns that clips my right leg just as I'm trying to drag it out of the way. It's only a glancing blow, and I'm so pumped up with adrenaline that I barely feel any pain, but I'm already off balance — tottering on one leg — so as the impact whips my other leg into the air, I kind of spin around and fall off the stile.

160

The path on the other side of the stile is so narrow that when I hit the ground — face-first — my head's actually hanging over the edge of the path, and although the darkness is so thick here that I can only see a few yards down the treacherously steep drop into the pitch-black depths of the valley below, there's something inside me, some kind of primitive bodily sense, that can physically *feel* the terrifying drop below me, and I can feel it turning my legs to jelly. I can feel something else too. There's a sense of "othersideness" here, a feeling that I've crossed over into something . . . a different world . . . a world where nightmares and reality are the same. And as I scramble desperately away from the edge, scrabbling backward on my hands and knees, I know without question that if I hesitate now — if I pause for even the tiniest moment — the fear will take hold of me and I won't be able to get moving again. So as I back into the fence and shakily get to my feet, I resist the almost irresistible urge to grab hold of the fence and cling on to it like a limpet, and I force myself to start shuffling off along the track.

It feels wrong, unnatural, as if I'm forcing myself to walk off the edge of a cliff, but the sound of more shouting — and barking — from the field helps me keep going. I know the monkems must have seen me going over the stile, so they're going to be coming after me, and the thought of that spurs me along too.

The snow on the path is deep and undisturbed, so I can't actually see the ground beneath it, and because there's no fence or railings, I can't see where the edge of the path is either. There's just a narrow white ribbon — the path — with the fence and the fields on one side, and a seemingly vast expanse of absolute blackness on the other. And the darkness on this side of the fence is so dense that I can barely see my hand in front of my face. So I'm staying as close to the fence as I can, continuously running my left hand along it, and I'm moving as fast as my useless right leg will let me, but not so fast that I risk falling over.

There's nothing in my head now. I'm not thinking about anything. I don't have a plan. I don't consciously know what I'm doing or where I'm going, and I don't seem to consciously care. I'm pure animal — driven by the urge to survive, existing from moment to moment — and the only thing that matters, the only thing there *is,* is living through the next second, the next step, the next breath . . .

I've never felt like this before.

The nightmarish fear is still there, still raging through me, and it's still as overwhelming as ever, but somehow it feels as if it doesn't belong to me anymore . . . or it does belong, but to a different me, a me that's down there — stumbling along the snow-covered dirt path, staying as close to the fence as he can, continuously running his left hand along it . . .

I can see him down there.

I can see him . . . wet and bedraggled, his haunted face streaked with mud, his right leg dragging through the snow, leaving a trail of blood behind him . . .

I see him glance awkwardly to his left as he hears the wail of an approaching siren, and I see the flashing blue lights that he sees, the pulsing strobe of emergency lights speeding up the road toward the village, and just for a moment I see the animal fear in his eyes . . .

But that's it.

I don't see him fall.

32

LIGHTS AT THE END OF THE WORLD

The two police officers had just finished dealing with a minor disturbance at the Holly Tree Inn when they saw the Vauxhall Corsa skidding around the corner, on the wrong side of the road, and speeding off up to the village. The headlights were off, all the windows were wide open, and Slade's "Merry Xmas Everybody" was booming out from the car radio.

Inside the car, Gordon was singing along at the top of his voice:

"IT'S CHRIIIISTMAAAASSSS!"

The two police officers — PCs Annie Hobbes and Mark Smith — ran across the pub parking lot, jumped into their car, and sped off after the Corsa.

It was 4:47 p.m.

Gordon was so entranced with the simple joy of singing that he didn't notice the police car for a while. He could hear the siren, but he thought it was coming from the radio, and even when he did finally see the flashing blue lights in his rearview mirror, he still didn't realize what they were. He saw them as electric-blue stars from another universe . . . Christmas stars . . . lights at the end of the world . . .

And then, quite suddenly, the wondrousness in his mind shut down, and a drug-crazed panic took over. Chaotic thoughts streamed through his head — *policepolicepolice oh no no no please no theycan't Ican'tstop if I stop I lose everythingeverything gottagetaway gottagetaway gottagetaway* — and as he put his foot down and sped up, the police car accelerated too.

Jenner and Dake both heard the siren at the same time, and they both knew right away that it wasn't an ambulance or a fire engine.

Dake immediately went over to the window and reached for the curtain, but Jenner told him to leave it.

"Yeah, but what if —?"

"Just leave it. They're not after us."

"How do you know?"

"No one knows we're here, do they?"

"What's-her-name does . . . the bank girl."

Jenner shook his head. "She won't have said anything. She can't rat us out without implicating herself, and she's not going to do that."

"She might have been drunk or something and told one of her friends . . . you know, bragging about it, trying to impress them . . ."

Jenner didn't answer. Dake was right, Kaylee did have a big mouth when she was drinking, and she had been on the booze today, and it wasn't difficult to imagine her boasting drunkenly about her "criminal connections," but Jenner wasn't going to admit to it.

"If the cops were on to us," he told Dake, "do you really think they'd come speeding up here with their lights and sirens blazing, letting us know they're coming?"

"No . . . I guess not."

"Exactly."

As the two of them stood there listening to the rapidly approaching siren, Grace and Shirley were listening to it too. They'd heard Jenner talking to Dake about it, and although they didn't understand the stuff about the "bank girl," it was obvious that Jenner didn't think the police siren had anything to do with them. But that didn't stop Grace and Shirley from hoping. They *had* to hope the police were coming, that any second now the siren would stop and a police car would screech to a halt outside the house, and they'd see the blue lights flashing through the curtains, and they'd hear the car doors opening, and a moment later clonking shut, and then . . .

A car sped past outside, its engine screaming as it raced

up into the village, and a few seconds later the wail of the siren drew level with the house, blue lights flashed across the curtains, and the pitch of the siren dropped as the police car shot past in pursuit of the speeding car.

"What did I tell you?" Jenner said casually, trying to hide his sense of relief.

Dake gave him a nod of acknowledgment.

And all Grace and Shirley could do was listen forlornly as the siren faded away into the distance, taking their hopes with it.

33

A WHIRLING DARKNESS

I don't know how it happens. One second I'm hobbling along the path, glancing to my left at the sound of a police siren coming up the road—and momentarily feeling that I'm somehow looking down on myself from above—and then all at once the ground isn't there anymore and I'm falling.

For a moment, all I feel is the tingled shock of my innards lurching upward as I drop down through the air, and then—before I've had time to work out what's happening—I hit solid ground again, landing heavily on my side, and then I kind of flip over a couple of times and start plummeting down the steep-sided slope of the valley—slipping and sliding, tumbling, rolling ... picking up speed all the time ... careening down through a whirling darkness of ground and sky and trees and snow and rocks and spinning limbs ... desperately trying to grab hold of something, my gloved (but cold and wet) fingers scrabbling blindly at the frozen ground . . . grasping at brambles, roots, half-buried rocks . . .

I don't know how long it takes before the slope finally starts to level out — it feels like I've been falling forever — but it's probably only been about ten seconds or so. The change in the gradient is quite gradual at first, but even when it really starts flattening out — becoming an almost walkable incline — the speed of my descent doesn't change. I've built up so much momentum that I just keep hurtling down . . . rolling over and over, skidding along on my back . . . clothes ripping . . . skin scraping . . . elbows and knees and my head bouncing off God-knows-what . . . but eventually I feel myself beginning to slow down, and instead of just tumbling and rolling uncontrollably, I somehow manage to get myself into a half-sitting-up position, so now I'm sliding down on my backside, with my elbows digging into the ground at my sides, and my legs stretched out in front of me. I'm still moving too fast to stop myself, and it still hurts a lot, but at least I've got *some* control, and I can see where I'm going at last . . .

I can see . . .

There's a light.

It's shining out at me from the wooded darkness ahead — a concentrated beam of bright white light — and as it slices toward me through the solid black air, I catch a fleeting glimpse of the area immediately in front of me. At the foot of the slope—just a few yards below me now—a short stretch of gently sloping ground leads down to a massive slab of granite embedded in the earth above a pathway. It's like a giant stone step—about ten yards long and five yards wide—and at the far end, it looks as if it just drops straight down to the pathway below. I can't actually see the ground directly below it, but I can see enough of the pathway on either side to guess that it's a drop of about one and a half yards.

On the other side of the snow-frosted path is the woods, which is where the light's coming from.

I see all this in an instant.

And an instant later, I hit the ground hard, feetfirst, and my forward momentum sends me staggering across the gentle slope and onto the granite slab, my arms windmilling as I try to stay on my feet, but it's always a losing battle, and just before I reach the end of the slab, I finally overbalance and go sprawling forward with my legs flying out behind me . . . and I know I'm not going to make it now . . . I can see the edge of the slab looming up at me as I stumble helplessly toward it, and I can see the path below . . . and at the very last moment—just as my right shoulder crashes down hard on the granite edge— I think I see the light in the woods moving toward me.

My right side clips the edge of the slab as I fall—a glancing impact that spins me over—so when I drop down to the path

I'm facing upward, and I land with a bone-jarring thump on my back that knocks all the wind out of me.

I don't move for a few moments, I just lie there with my eyes closed, gasping for breath, trying to work out if I'm seriously hurt anywhere or just battered and bruised all over.

I hear something then, a close-up sound, right next to my head — a heavy footstep crunching in the snow — and when I open my eyes all I can see is a blinding light shining down into my face.

As I raise my hands to shield my eyes from the dazzling light, I hear a voice from above. It's a male voice, and there's a smirking menace to it that makes my blood run cold.

"Well, well," it says, "what have we got here?"

34

THE HILLBILLY

Everything hurts as I cautiously ease myself up into a sitting position, and although I'm desperate to get to my feet and get away from whoever spoke to me — and who's still standing over me with a flashlight — my head's spinning so much that even the process of sitting up has made me feel nauseous and dizzy, so all I can do for now is kind of shuffle over a bit and sit with my back against the granite slab.

The flashlight's still blinding me, so I still can't see who's there, but just as I'm raising my hand to shield my eyes again, the flashlight is suddenly lowered. It takes a little while for the burning bright afterimages to clear from my eyes, but once they're gone, I can finally see what I'm up against.

There are two of them.

The one who spoke to me is a skinny monkem in his early twenties. He has nasty little eyes, whiskery tufts of beard on his chin, and his skin is so pale that it looks almost transparent. He's wearing a camouflage jacket and a matching peaked cap with earflaps, and his cheap denim jeans are tucked into ankle-high boots. The most noticeable thing about him though, the thing I can't take my eyes off, is the rifle he's holding in his hands. It's real, no doubt about it, and as I sit there staring at it, dazed and confused, an unwanted image of the old-monkem-lady's rifle flashes into my mind, and I can see it now for what it really was — a walking stick . . . not one of the old-fashioned wooden ones, but a longish metal one, the kind that comes up to your elbow and has an arm clip and a sticky-out handle . . .

I blink hard and shake my head, clearing the useless image from my mind, and I refocus on the skinny monkem in front of me, and the rifle that definitely *isn't* a walking stick in his hands.

Now that he isn't shining the flashlight directly into my face, I can see that it's attached to the rifle. I can see his companion now too. He's standing next to him, a couple of feet to his right, but he's hanging back a little, as if he knows his place. He's roughly the same age as the one with the rifle, maybe a bit younger, and their faces are so similar that I wouldn't be surprised if they're brothers. The younger one isn't so pale and gaunt, though, and although he looks kind of tough — and he's quite a bit bigger and heftier than the other one — he doesn't have the same sense of menace about him. He's dressed almost identically to his brother/companion, but without the hat. He's got a canvas bag slung over his shoulder, and dangling from his left hand is the limp body of a small brown deer. It's only a little thing — not much bigger than a small dog — and it's hanging from the big monkem's hand by its tiny horns, swinging gently in his grip. From the way he's holding it — as casually (and mindlessly) as if it was a bag full of trash — it's obvious that the dead animal means absolutely nothing to him. I can't see where it's been shot, but blood's oozing from somewhere . . . the red drops dripping slowly from a delicate hoof, peppering the snow with a ragged circle of bright pink spots.

The skinny monkem moves his flashlight then, directing the beam at my injured right foot. It's the first time I've seen it clearly, and the sight of it turns my stomach. It's a complete mess. The big toe's split open, the nail hanging off, and there's blood everywhere . . . all over my foot, my toes, my ankle . . .

"That looks painful," the monkem says.

There's no sympathy or curiosity in his voice, just a slight mocking edge, and there's something in his eyes, something about the way he's looking at me, that makes me think of a cruel child poking a damaged insect with a stick.

"You ought to get that looked at," he goes on. "Probably needs a couple of stitches."

"Yeah . . ." I mutter, lowering my eyes and gazing at the ground.

"Yeah?"

I look up at him, not sure what he means, and when I see the blankness in his staring eyes, I know he doesn't mean anything. He's just saying something — it doesn't matter what — to get a reaction. He knows I'm scared, and he likes it. I'm his damaged insect, and he's going to carry on poking me with his stick until he gets tired of it, or until I stop moving, whichever comes first.

I start getting to my feet then. I still feel dizzy and sick, and I don't doubt that standing up's going to make me feel even worse, but if that's what it takes to get away from this hillbilly-psycho-monkem and his sidekick/brother, that's what I'm going to do.

I've barely even moved, though — only just starting to lean forward and push myself up — when the hillbilly takes a step toward me and prods me in the chest with the rifle barrel. It's not a hard prod, and it doesn't really hurt that much, but because I'm already off balance, it's enough to knock me back against the granite slab and then back down onto my backside. When I immediately try to get up again, the hillbilly gives me another poke with his rifle, only this time it's more of a jab than a prod, and it *does* hurt. As I slump back down to the ground again, he moves closer and presses the rifle barrel into my chest, pinning me back against the slab.

I look up at him.

He's smiling at me.

It's the ugliest smile I've ever seen.

"Where's your manners?" he says.

"What?"

"I was talking to you. You can't just get up and go when someone's in the middle of talking to you. It's bad manners."

I can't remember if he *was* talking to me or not, but I know it doesn't matter. All that matters right now is that he's holding a rifle to my chest.

"Sorry . . ." I mutter, trying to sound genuine. "I didn't realize you hadn't finished talking . . . I didn't mean to be —"

"What's your name?"

"What?"

"You heard me. What's your name?"

"Elliot."

"Elliot?" he sneers. "What kind of name is that?"

"It's not any kind," I mumble. "It's just —"

"Shut up."

His voice has changed, it's suddenly harsh and urgent, and when I glance up at him I see that he's not looking at me anymore. He's staring upward, his hunter's eyes scanning the path at the top of the slope. Something's alerted him, and a moment later I hear it too — the faint sound of voices . . . male voices . . . coming along the path . . .

They're too distant to recognize, but I'm pretty sure it's the four monkems from the field, and they're definitely getting closer now, their voices carrying down through the icy black air into the valley . . .

The hillbilly turns off his flashlight, plunging us into sudden darkness, and a moment later he's crouching down next to me, holding a hunting knife to my throat. I can feel the tip of the blade pricking my skin, and as he leans in close to me, his face almost touching mine, I can smell the stomach-stink of his breath.

"You make a sound," he whispers, "and I'll cut your throat."

35

One Lost Soul

The four men were standing around a caved-in hole in the path — two on either side — and as they swept their flashlights over the surrounding area, it wasn't hard to figure out what had happened. The boy had clearly come along the path — his blood-spotted trail in the snow was unmissable — and it was equally obvious from the undisturbed snow on the other side of the hole that he hadn't gone any farther. The ground must have been weakened here for some reason — maybe a badger or a fox had burrowed in under the path — and the weak point must have given way when the boy stepped onto it. There was very little snow on the steep-sided slope of the valley, so it wasn't quite so easy to track the boy's descent, but there was still enough evidence to show that he'd fallen — scuffs and skid tracks in the dirt, broken branches — and besides, where else could he have gone?

"I told you not to bring your damn dog," Davey Price said to Geoff Crocker. "Olive told us the kid's scared of dogs."

They were both gazing down into the valley, sweeping their flashlights around, searching for any signs of life in the darkness. Molly the dog was sitting beside Geoff Crocker, and he had her leash gripped tightly in his hand.

"What was I supposed to do?" he said to Davey. "I couldn't just tie her up to the gate, could I? And anyway, I thought she could help us."

"Yeah, right. She was a great help, wasn't she?"

"I was only trying to —"

"Hey," one of the other two said, "this isn't the time for arguing, okay?" His name was Athel Wright. He glared at Davey and Geoff for a moment, then peered down into the valley. "There's a young boy down there somewhere. He might be seriously hurt — in fact, I'd be surprised if he isn't — and even if he's not hurt, he's scared, he's cold, and he's alone in the darkness." He looked over at Davey and Geoff. "We need to find him as soon as possible."

They both nodded.

Davey put his flashlight in his pocket, cupped his hands to his mouth, and started shouting down into the valley. *"HEY! HELLO? ARE YOU DOWN THERE? CAN YOU HEAR ME?"* He paused, listening. Then tried again. *"IT'S OKAY, DON'T BE*

179

SCARED . . . WE JUST WANT TO HELP YOU . . ." He paused and listened again, but there was still no response.

"We need to get down there," he said.

"It's too steep here," Athel observed. "We'll either have to head back along the path and cut down one of the tracks where the slope's not so steep, or else keep going this way, take the steps that lead down to the river, and then come back along the path through the woods."

"Which way's quicker?" Geoff asked.

Athel thought about it for a moment, then said, "I think it's probably best to go back the way we came and cut down into the woods."

"We could split up," Davey suggested. "Two of us go back, the other two go forward."

Athel shook his head. "We stay together. One lost soul's enough on a night like this. We don't want to lose anyone else."

Before they left, Davey called down into the valley again. *"WE'RE NOT LEAVING, OKAY? WE JUST NEED TO FIND A WAY DOWN. WE'LL BE WITH YOU AS SOON AS WE CAN."*

36

PSYCHO-STINK

"WE'RE NOT LEAVING, OKAY? WE JUST NEED TO FIND A
WAY DOWN. WE'LL BE WITH YOU AS SOON AS WE CAN."

There's a part of me that hears the shouted voices drifting
down into the valley, and it knows where they're coming from
and what they mean, but it's only a very small part. The rest of
me — the most of me — is in a different world now, a world of
howling demons and insatiable beasts whirling around inside
me, getting bigger and bigger all the time ... bigger, faster,
stronger, hungrier ...

The Moloxetine's worn off.

The lock on the cage has cracked and crumbled ...

The door has swung open ...

The beast is free.

I can feel it raging inside me, pumping raw fear into my
heart, my blood, my flesh ... sickening me, emptying me ...

shaking me to my bones . . . and I can taste its stinking breath rising up into my throat . . .

But it's not pure fear.

There's something else there too, something that's almost indistinguishable from fear, but with one crucial difference — instead of every cell in my body screaming at me to run away, this time they're raging at me to fight.

I *am* the beast. Its fury is mine.

And as the hillbilly crouches there beside me, still holding his knife to my throat — and still breathing his psycho-stink into my face — I feel the crazed fury taking me out of myself, lifting me up into the darkness . . . and now I can see him again, the me that's down there, and I can see the monster squatting down next to him too. And the other one, the sidekick/brother, standing motionless in the dark, the dead deer hanging from his hand . . . I can see him as well. But he's nothing.

The monster's the one.

He's got his knife in his right hand and his rifle in his left, and he's watching the flashlights at the top of the slope, watching intently with his animal eyes as they head back along the path, back the way they came, and he knows exactly what the men are doing. *WE'RE NOT LEAVING, OKAY? WE JUST NEED TO FIND A WAY DOWN.* They're going to cut down one of the tracks where the slope's not so steep, then double back along the path through the woods.

The monster smiles to himself.

He's happy.

He likes the thrill of the hunt. It doesn't matter to him if he's the hunter or the hunted, it's the raw exhilaration that does it for him — the rush of adrenaline, the primal vitality, the sense of kill-or-be-killed — it makes him feel alive.

He likes having power over things too. Animals, people . . . he doesn't care. They're all the same to him. He likes to frighten things, hurt things, kill things. It makes him feel good. And that's the whole point of everything, isn't it? Making yourself feel good. What else *is* there?

I follow his sick-eyed gaze as he glances at the other-me beside him.

The other-me's a mess — his dirt-streaked face covered in cuts and scratches, his sodden clothes ripped and torn, his right glove missing, fingernails torn and bleeding, his bare foot badly swollen. The bruising on his foot is an ugly mixture of purpled-black and yellow, and in places the skin is dead-white. The other-me's complexion is almost bloodless too, his face white beneath the dirt and mud, and the eyes . . .

The other-me's eyes.

The moment I look at them, they blink, and in an instant, they change from the desperate eyes of a frightened animal — staring, haunted — to the cold hard eyes of a survivor. As well as seeing this sudden change, I can feel it too. We're together. I can feel what we feel, in our head and our heart . . . and I can feel the heavy rock in our hand. I can feel it right now, and I can feel us finding it a few moments ago — our hand cautiously scouring the ground, looking for anything to use as a weapon, our fingertips lighting upon the ice-filmed rock . . . then taking hold of it, feeling its size and weight — all the time making sure the hillbilly doesn't know what we're doing — and then, once we're satisfied that the rock is big and heavy enough, but not too big or heavy to get a good grip on, all we have to do is keep hold of it, keep still, keep our face blank, and wait for the right moment.

We don't have to wait very long.

The hillbilly-monster is waiting too, waiting for the flash-lights to disappear into the darkness. And when they do — and after he's carried on watching for another minute or two to make sure they don't come back — he slips the hunting knife back into the sheath on his belt, transfers the rifle to his right hand, and with his left hand turns on the flashlight.

We act instantly, dropping our left shoulder and swinging our right arm as hard and fast as we can, and before the hillbilly has a chance to do or say anything, we hammer the rock into his head.

37

A Thing of Cold Silence

The other-me is something else now.

Something else.

A thing of cold silence, dead in the heart . . . not me. I'm still up here, looking down . . . watching this thing-that-isn't-quite-me-anymore . . . watching as it drops the bloodied rock and picks up the hillbilly's rifle, not even glancing at the monster slumped in the snow beside him, not caring if it's dead or alive. The other-me just gets to its feet, holding the rifle at its waist, and turns to the sidekick/brother.

The flashlight on the rifle is still turned on, and as the other-me levels the rifle at the sidekick/brother, the white beam lights up his fear-stricken face. Without taking his wide-open eyes off the other-me, he takes a hesitant step back, half stumbling over something, and raises his hands in the air. He's so frozen with fear that he doesn't realize he's still holding the dead deer, and it just hangs there from his raised hand, swinging lifelessly in the black-and-white air.

The snow's started falling again, fine and light in the dark.

"Lay it down," the other-me says to the sidekick/brother.

"What?"

"The deer . . . lay it down on the ground, and do it carefully. If you drop it, I'll shoot you."

The sidekick/brother doesn't understand — *it's dead . . . it's nothing . . . what does it matter if I drop it or not?* — but when a crazy kid with a loaded rifle tells you to do something, you don't ask questions, do you? You just do what he says. So the sidekick/brother slowly stoops down, still holding the deer by its horns, and lays it carefully in the snow.

"Now turn around," the other-me says when the sidekick/brother has straightened up again.

"What? Why . . . ? What are you going to —?"

"Do it."

The other-me has raised the rifle to its shoulder and is aiming it directly at the sidekick/brother's head. The sidekick/brother can see the cold-blooded truth in the other-me's eyes — it *will* shoot him if he doesn't turn around — and he knows he has no choice. His mouth is bone-dry now, his throat so tight he can barely breathe, and as he awkwardly shuffles around, he can feel the terrible thud of the bullet hitting him in the back . . . he can physically *feel* it . . . it's there, right there, between his shoulder blades . . . and he can see himself collapsing to the ground . . . legs buckling . . . body crumpling . . . dropping dead into the snow . . . like a gutshot deer.

The other-me waits until the sidekick/brother is fully turned around, then it pauses for a moment, looking down at the hillbilly-monster's boots. They're large, at least a size nine or ten, which normally would be far too big for it, but its right foot is so swollen now that even a size ten would be too small for it.

The other-me takes a final look at the sidekick/brother. It sees him standing there, his raised hands trembling, his hunched shoulders rigid with tension—braced for the terrible thud of the bullet—and the other-me knows it doesn't have to worry about him. He won't try to follow us . . .

Us?

It?

Him?

Me?

I don't know anymore.

I don't know what's happening to me.

38

GREAT BLACK TREES

It's cold and dark, and I'm limping along the pathway through the woods, using the rifle as a walking stick. My right foot's useless, just a throbbing mess of flesh and bone. Everything else hurts too . . . every cell in my body. And I'm *so* tired . . . just so incredibly tired . . .

There's a flashlight in my left hand (I must have taken it off the rifle), and in its beam I can see the lightness of the falling snow, and I can see the white-topped branches of great black trees, and up ahead of me I can see an endless climb of rough wooden steps leading up the steep-sided slope to the narrow dirt track at the top . . . and then another pathway appears beside me, running parallel to this one, and on that pathway there's a wolf . . . a big bad wolf . . . and the red-hooded figure of a little girl carrying a basket . . . and as I watch them walking along their pathway through the woods, I hear a voice from a thousand years away

shake it . . .

like this

and all at once the ground tilts beneath my feet and a blizzard suddenly erupts out of nowhere, a great white whirlwind of giant snowflakes swirling and tumbling all around me . . .

And then I'm back in my room with Ellamay, and I'm staring at the snow globe on my shelf, and she's saying, *What is it, Elliot?*

"Nothing," I tell her, looking away from the snow globe.

What did you see?

"What do you mean?"

You know what I mean. What did you see just now in the snow globe?

"Nothing . . ."

She knows I'm lying. She always knows.

Just tell me, she says quietly. *What did you see?*

"It was snowing . . . like someone had shaken it up. That's what made me look at it. And I saw something . . . or I thought I did."

In the snow?

"In the whole thing."

What was it, Elliot? What did you see?

"This," I tell her now. "I saw this."

189

The bedraggled figure limping along the pathway, the falling snow, the white-topped branches of great black trees, the endless climb of rough wooden steps leading up to a narrow dirt track at the top of the slope . . .

I saw it all in a timeless moment.

And I'm seeing it all again now. But this time, I'm not seeing it in *my* snow globe, the one I keep on the shelf in my bedroom, I'm seeing it in Auntie Shirley's snow globe, the one she keeps on the windowsill in her living room, and at the same time I'm seeing it from both inside the globe and inside my head . . .

I'm there, limping along the path through the falling snow toward the wooden steps . . .

And I'm here.

I don't seem to know why I'm heading toward the steps, or where they go, or what I have to do when I get to the top . . . but for now that doesn't seem to matter. All that matters, and all I know for sure, is that I have to climb them.

39

Do They Know It's Christmas?

"What time is it now?"

"Will you stop asking me what time it is, for Christ's sake? Haven't you got a watch?"

Dake shook his head. "I use the clock on my cell phone."

"So use it."

"I can't, can I?"

"Why not?"

"The battery's dead."

Jenner sighed, giving Dake a withering glare. "You're unbelievable . . . you really are. I mean, you knew we were doing this today, didn't you?"

"Yeah . . ." He shrugged. "So what?"

"So why didn't you make sure your phone was fully charged this morning? *That's* what."

"I did. I plugged in the charger last night."

"Yeah? So how come it's dead now?"

"I don't know . . ." Dake paused, looking a bit sheepish. "I suppose I might have forgotten to connect the cable . . ."

Jenner rolled his eyes in exasperation. "You *might* have forgotten . . . ?"

"Yeah . . . I mean, I'm not saying I did . . . not for sure . . . but it's an easy thing to do, isn't it?"

"For a moron it is, yeah."

"I'm not a moron."

"No?" Jenner sneered. "You could have fooled me."

Across the room, Shirley and Grace were just sitting there, slumped against the radiator. Both of them were staring down at the floor, and both were thinking about their sons. There were tears in their eyes, and they both wished they could stop thinking about their sons, stop imagining the worst, just for a while, but they knew they couldn't — not now, not ever.

Wishes never come true.

"Yeah, so anyway . . ." Dake said.

"What?"

Dake grinned. "What time is it?"

Gordon hadn't escaped from the police car yet, and he was beginning to wonder if he ever would. But the funny thing was that although he was still perfectly aware that this was a seriously bad situation, and although the thought of getting caught (and losing everything) still filled him with a sickening dread, he had to admit that part of him — an unfamiliar part — was actually really enjoying all this.

He still wanted to get away from the police car, though.

He thought he'd succeeded five minutes earlier just as he was approaching the moors. A long bend in the road had momentarily put him out of sight of the police car, and when he'd seen the track on his left, he'd immediately hit the brakes and swung the skidding Corsa off the road and onto the track. The snow was thick here, and the ground beneath it was rutted with tank tracks. Gordon just about managed to keep the car going, and as it lumped and bucked across the uneven ground, he leaned forward, moving right up close to the windshield, and squinted out to see where he was going. There was just enough light from the pale scythe of the moon to see a locked gate up ahead, barring his way, and the warning sign fixed to it — TANKS TURNING.

He swung the Corsa to the left, taking it off the track and onto what he hoped was the flatter surface of the moor land next to it, and then — just as the headlights of the police car were appearing around the bend in the road — he quickly turned off the engine.

The police car sped past — lights and siren still blazing — and Gordon watched as the flashing blue light raced away across the moor, leaving an electric-blue trail behind it, until finally he couldn't see it anymore. He waited another minute or two, just to be on the safe side, then he started the engine, gave it a few revs, and hoped to God that the Corsa wasn't stuck in the snow.

It wasn't.

The wheels spun for a few heart-sinking moments, the car sliding uncontrollably to one side, but when Gordon put his foot down, cautiously giving it a bit more power, the wheels suddenly got a grip and the Corsa lunged forward.

Gordon was feeling pretty pleased with himself as he reached the end of the track and rejoined the road—he'd outwitted the cops, he'd saved himself from a *very* tricky situation, and now, at last, he was on his way home.

You need to think about what you're going to tell Mother, he told himself as he turned right onto the road. *You can't tell her what really happened, can you? She'd go ballistic. You'll have to make something up. Tell her that—*

"Damn!"

A distant blue light had appeared in the rearview mirror, and when Gordon twisted around and looked out of the rear window, he saw the flashing blue light and the glaring headlights of the police car cresting a rise in the road about a hundred yards back. The siren started whooping, and Gordon could see that the patrol car was really moving, streaking through the snow like a rocket.

He swore again, this time using a word he'd never used before in his whole life.

He was so surprised at himself that for a moment or two he was too stunned to do anything. He just sat there, his mouth half open, unable to believe not only *what* he'd just said, but the passion with which he'd said it. And then, quite suddenly, he broke into a manic smile and reached down to turn the radio on.

The song booming out of the speakers was Band Aid's "Do They Know It's Christmas?," and as the Corsa raced away, its wheels spinning and its back end sliding from side to side, Gordon threw his head back and sang along with all his heart.

40

MY SKEWERED SKULL

We had to do it.

"Do what?"

Hit the hillbilly with a rock. We had no choice.

"I know."

It was him or us.

"I know."

We don't have to feel bad about it.

"I don't."

Really?

"Yeah."

We're on the wooden steps now, and although we've only just begun the steep climb up, I'm already so exhausted that I know I'm never going to make it to the top.

"I'm done," I gasp, stopping to get my breath. "I can't go any farther."

Yes, you can.

"I can't . . ." I gaze upward at the dizzying height of the steps, and from down here, it looks as if they go on forever — disappearing into the darkness and reaching all the way up to the glass sky and beyond . . .

"The glass sky . . . ?"

What?

"Nothing." I bend over, hands on knees, and try to get some air into my lungs.

"I can't do it," I say. "It's too far."

You can take one more step, can't you? Just one more . . . ?

"What's the point?"

Just try it, okay? For me.

I sigh heavily, then — using the rifle to hoist myself up — I take another laboriously painful step.

See? That wasn't so difficult, was it?

"It was just one step."

They're all just one step.

I'm too tired to argue. I put my head down and start climbing the never-ending steps again.

You know it wasn't a gunshot, don't you? Ella says.

"What?"

The old monkems in the car, you know . . . the old-monkem-lady with the walking stick that wasn't a rifle? Ella grins. *You heard a bang, and you thought it was a gunshot, remember?*

"Yeah."

It wasn't a gunshot. It was the car backfiring.

"I know."

Silence.

    I keep going.

    Keep climbing.

    One impossible step at a time.

What does Whitby have to do with Little Red Riding Hood anyway?

"What?"

The snow globe . . .

"What about it?"

It doesn't make sense.

"Of course it doesn't. None of this makes sense."

Well, yeah, but the thing about the snow globe, the thing I've never understood, is why it has Little Red Riding Hood in it.

"Why shouldn't it?"

Because Shirley got it from a souvenir shop in Whitby, and as far as I know, Little Red Riding Hood doesn't have anything to do with Whitby. I mean, there's no connection at all, is there?

"How do you know there's not?"

Whitby's famous for Dracula, not Little Red Riding Hood.

"Maybe Shirley didn't get it from Whitby. Maybe she got it from wherever Little Red Riding Hood comes from."

Little Red Riding Hood's a character in a fairy tale. She doesn't come from anywhere.

"Right. And you think Dracula's real, do you?"

You know what I mean.

We lapse into silence again for a while, and as I carry on heaving myself up the everlasting steps — one by one by one . . . each step getting higher all the time, while my body gets heavier and heavier — I *think* I'm thinking about the snow globe . . . trying to work out why I keep thinking about it, why it keeps coming back to me — but after a while, I realize that I'm not thinking about it at all . . . I'm not thinking about anything . . . my head's just an empty skull, a sphere of bone skewered on top of a spine . . .

But then, I ask myself, if it *is* empty, if there really *is* nothing inside my head, where are *these* thoughts coming from?

And now my otherness rises up through my spine and out through my skewered skull into the cold black air above me, and as I look down — for a measureless moment — I see the red-hooded figure of a little girl struggling up the steps, using a rifle as a walking stick . . . and I can see that her right foot's useless, just a throbbing mess of flesh and bone, and she's hurting all over, and she's *so* tired . . . just so incredibly tired . . . and as I watch her heaving herself up the wooden steps — one by relentless one . . . each step getting higher

all the time, her body getting heavier and heavier . . . I hear
her voice

Elliot?

and she becomes me again.

Do you want to know something else that doesn't make sense?

"No."

It's got nothing to do with the snow globe.

"I don't care what it is. I don't want to hear it."

It won't take long.

"I know what you're doing."

What do you mean?

"All this talking . . . it's just a diversion, a distraction. You're
trying to take my mind off everything else."

What mind?

"Yeah, very funny."

*All right, I admit it. You're right. I should have known it wouldn't
work. You were always too smart for me.*

"Yeah, well, it *was* pretty obvious."

*There's no distracting you, is there? You always know exactly what's
going on.*

"I wouldn't say that . . ."

Look around.

"What?"

Open your eyes and look around.

I didn't even know my eyes were closed, and when I open

them and look around, I realize that I'm not climbing the steps anymore. I've climbed them. I'm standing at the top of the steps, leaning on my rifle-walking-stick, breathing heavily . . . and as I gaze back down the steps, and I see them disappearing into the bottomless darkness below, I know I can't have climbed them. It's impossible. There are too many of them, they're too steep. I couldn't have made it all the way up there, not in a million years.

I see the lights then.

Down in the woods, away to my right . . . faint lights, flashing intermittently through the trees.

The four monkems from the field.

"Yeah."

They're still quite a long way away.

"Yeah."

They'll find the hillbilly.

"If he's still there."

I don't think he'll have gone anywhere.

"We had to do it."

I know.

I turn to my left then and look along the snow-covered dirt track stretching out ahead of me. I can just make out a slight graying in the darkness not too far along the path, a patch of blackness that's not quite as black as everything else.

It's the field at the back of Shirley's house. It's not so dark there. It's got the lights from the road, the lights from the houses . . . there's probably a stile into the field at the end of the path. That's what you can see. The lighter patch is where the stile leads into the field.

It's hard to tell how far away it is — and I don't trust my senses anymore anyway — but something in the pit of my belly tells me it's fairly close.

"Ready?"

Yeah.

"All right, let's go."

We set off along the track, and this time, before every step, I prod the ground in front of me with the rifle-walking-stick, making sure it's safe to walk on. If I fall down into the valley again, I know — without a shadow of doubt — that I'll never get out.

Do you know what we're doing now?

"Yeah."

Tell me.

"We're going to Shirley's."

What for?

"To find Mum."

41

THREE THINGS

Police Officer Annie Hobbes had called in the Corsa's registration number from the patrol car at the Holly Tree Inn, and by the time her partner, Officer Mark Smith, had realized that the fleeing car was no longer ahead of them on the road across the moors, they already knew who the Corsa was registered to, which meant that as long as it hadn't been stolen—and there were no reports that it had been—and as long as the driver *was* the registered owner, then they knew who he was and where he lived.

"Any outstanding warrants on him?" Smith asked Hobbes as he turned the patrol car around and sped off back along the road.

"He's clean," Hobbes said. "Not even a parking ticket." She glanced over her shoulder, looking back through the rear windshield. "Are you sure—?"

"There he is!"

Hobbes quickly turned around again, and as the patrol car lurched over a rise in the road, she saw the Corsa up ahead. It was about a hundred yards away, speeding back along the road, away from them, its wheels spinning and its back end sliding from side to side.

Hobbes reached for the radio clipped to her collar.

"Charlie Three Zero," she said into it. "Suspect vehicle now heading east, repeat east, on Grinton Lane. In pursuit."

A moment later, a voice crackled out from the radio.

"Received. Charlie Three Four is approaching the suspect's address, requesting advice on how to proceed."

Hobbes glanced at Smith. "What do you think?"

"Tell them to wait when they get there, lights and sirens off," he said. "We'll have a better idea what to do when we find out which way he goes at the junction."

Hobbes nodded and spoke into her radio. "Charlie Three Four?"

"Go ahead."

"Where are you, Griff?"

"Just coming into the village."

"Wait when you get to the house, okay? Lights and sirens off."

"Received."

*

Griff Beattie immediately switched off the siren and the emergency lights, and his partner in the driver's seat, Rick Tarn, took his foot off the accelerator and slowed the car to a steady thirty miles per hour.

"Which one is it?" he asked Beattie as the houses came into view.

Beattie leaned forward, peering through the windshield. "I think it's that one," he said, pointing to a house on the right-hand side of the road. "The first one, the one with the red door." He looked down at the notebook in his lap, checked the address he'd been given, then looked back at the house. "Yeah, that's definitely it."

Tarn glanced over at the house, then began looking around for a parking space. Both sides of the road were lined with parked cars, and the only gap Tarn could see was on the left-hand side between a Škoda Fabia and a Land Rover. The only possible problem was that it was directly opposite the house, and Tarn wasn't sure if that mattered or not.

"Did Annie say we had to keep out of sight?" he asked Beattie, slowing the car to a crawl.

Beattie shook his head. "Just wait."

"So do you think we're all right parking here?"

"I don't see why not." He gazed out through the windshield at the lines of cars parked along the road. "It doesn't look as if we've got much choice anyway, does it?"

Tarn nodded, then began maneuvering the car into the space behind the Land Rover.

"Did you hear that?" Dake said.

"Hear what?"

"Another siren."

"What siren? I didn't hear anything."

"I'm sure I heard it," Dake said, crossing over to the front window. "It sounded like it was —"

"What are you doing?"

Dake reached for the curtain. "I just want to check —"

"Leave it, for Christ's sake! I already told you —"

"Shit!"

"What is it?"

Dake had inched the curtain open and peeked through the gap, and a split second later he'd yanked it shut again and quickly stepped back, his eyes wide and his face drained of color.

"What *is* it?" Jenner repeated, his voice calm but urgent.

"Cops . . ."

"Where?"

"There! Right outside . . . they're right *there*!"

"At the door?"

"*What?*"

"Are the cops at the door?"

Dake shook his head. "Across the road . . . they're parked across the road, right behind the Land Rover."

"They're in a car?"

"Yeah."

"Marked or unmarked?"

"Marked . . . a patrol car."

"Just the one?"

"I only saw one."

"How many in the car?"

"I don't know . . . as soon as I saw it I shut the curtain." As Jenner came over to him, Dake's staring eyes were bulging with panic. "What are we going to *do*? What the *hell* are we going to do?"

"Just calm down, okay?"

"Calm *down*?"

"Listen, Dake —"

"You're seriously telling me to calm *down*?"

"They don't know we're here."

Dake froze. "What? What do you mean?"

"Think about it. If the police knew we were here, if they knew what we were doing, they wouldn't just send out a single patrol car, would they? If they were on to us, there'd be dozens of cops out there — hostage teams, snipers, negotiators . . ."

"Maybe there *are* dozens of them out there," Dake said. "I

mean, they wouldn't be out in the open, would they? They'd be keeping themselves out of sight."

"Yeah, and they wouldn't park a patrol car right across the road from us either, would they?"

It took Dake a little while to work out what Jenner was saying, and when he finally got it — slowly nodding to himself — some of the fear and panic left him. Some, but not all. There might not be dozens of armed police out there, but there *was* a patrol car, and whatever it was doing there — whether it had anything to do with them or not — it wasn't a good situation.

"Check out the back," Jenner said to him, moving over to the wall next to the front window.

"I'm not going out there."

"Just take a look through the window."

"What for?"

"Anything. Just do it, okay?"

As Dake went over to the back window, Jenner cautiously opened a tiny gap in the curtains and looked out. The patrol car was parked exactly where Dake had said — right across the road, directly opposite the house, between a Škoda and the stolen Land Rover. The headlights were off, the engine wasn't running. Jenner could see that there were two of them in the car, but the nearest streetlight was at least twenty yards away, and in the dim light he couldn't make out much detail. They were both in uniform, he was sure of that, and so far — from what he could see — there was nothing to suggest they knew about him and Dake. There was nothing to suggest they didn't either. But then headlights suddenly appeared, the twin beams of a car coming down the road, and just for a second the face of the cop in the driver's seat was clearly visible. He looked away almost immediately, quickly turning his head to the left, but he wasn't quite fast enough. Jenner had seen his eyes. He'd seen them staring hard at the house . . .

They knew.

There was no doubt in Jenner's mind.

They knew about him and Dake.

He closed the gap in the curtains and stepped back. Across the room, Dake had pulled back the edge of the curtain and was peering out through the window.

"See anything?" Jenner said.

"No," Dake said, letting go of the curtain edge and turning to Jenner. "Are the cops still out there?"

"Yeah . . ."

"Still in their car?"

"Yeah."

"I think you're right."

"About what?"

"Well, they wouldn't be just sitting out there if they knew

about us, would they? They must be out there for another reason. It's the only thing that makes sense." Dake smiled nervously. "We're going to be all right, aren't we?"

"Yeah," Jenner said, "we're going to be fine."

There were three things bothering Shirley. First, she *really* needed to pee. She'd been desperate to go for the last couple of hours, and it was getting to the stage now where her bloated bladder wasn't just uncomfortable, it was really painful. She'd tried telling the two men that she needed to go to the lavatory, grunting and mumbling through the tape over her mouth, but they'd either not understood her or they simply didn't care. She was damned if she was going to suffer the embarrassment of wetting herself, though, so she'd just resigned herself to being in pain.

The second thing bothering her was the curtain in the back window. When Dake had finished looking out of the window, he hadn't closed the curtain properly. The edge he'd been holding back had snagged on the heavy blue vase on the windowsill — as it quite often did — and Dake either hadn't noticed or couldn't be bothered to do anything about it. It bothered Shirley, though. In fact, it bothered her a lot. Stupid little things like that had always bothered her — cutlery being in the wrong place in the cutlery drawer, cans of food facing the wrong way in the cupboard . . . all kinds of meaningless things. She knew it was totally irrational to worry about them, and that nothing bad would happen if she *didn't* rearrange the cans or close the curtain properly, but the way Shirley saw it was that it was a lot easier to just accept her little foibles than to put herself through the hell of trying to get rid of them.

The third thing bothering her was the sudden change in Jenner's demeanor. She'd noticed it when he'd turned back from the front window, and she'd heard it in his voice when he'd told Dake they were "going to be fine," and as he stood there now — staring at the floor, absentmindedly scratching at a rash on his chin — she knew she wasn't mistaken. Something had changed in him. It wasn't an obvious change, and Shirley was fairly sure that Dake hadn't noticed it, but there was no question in her mind that whatever Jenner had seen outside — and it had to be something to do with the police car they'd been talking about — it had suddenly made him realize not just the enormity of what he was doing, but also the subsequent level of punishment he'd face if he was caught, and what he might have to do to avoid being caught and punished.

He'd looked up from the floor now and was gazing over at Shirley and Grace, and Shirley could see the cold calculation in his eyes. He didn't *want* to kill them — not for their sakes, but simply because it would make things worse for him — but if it came down to a choice between their lives and his . . . ?

He wouldn't hesitate for a moment.

He'd do what he had to do.

Shirley knew it. And as Jenner looked away from her and began talking to Dake, and she turned to her sister beside her, she could tell right away from the look in Grace's eyes that she knew it too.

42

Just Dead

I hear the siren just as I'm going over the stile into the field at the back of Shirley's house. It sounds like it's coming up the road into the village, and I wonder briefly if it's the same police car (or fire engine or ambulance) I heard earlier or a different one. The siren I heard before was also coming up the road, so unless that police car (or fire engine or ambulance) had gone back down the road with its siren off, I think this is probably a different one. And as I start struggling up and across the field to my left, heading for the backs of the houses, I also wonder (just as briefly) if either siren has anything to do with Mum or Shirley or me.

It's possible, I guess . . .

It's possible.

But that's as far as I can go with it. I feel so dead now, physically and mentally, that the only thing I can think about — the only thing I *have* to think about — is the exhausting and agonizing (and at times seemingly impossible) process of walking. Every single step has become a grueling trial of body and mind, and with every single step the trial's getting harder and harder.

I keep going . . .

You can take one more step, can't you? Just one more . . . ?

What's the point?

Just try it, okay? For me.

Keep trying . . .

See? That wasn't so difficult, was it?

It was just one step.

They're all just one step . . .

I don't know how long it's been since the siren went quiet, and I have no idea if it faded away into the distance or stopped suddenly. All I know is that after a while — a minute? two minutes? — I realize it's not there anymore. And at the same time I also realize that I'm not walking across the field anymore. I've reached the rickety old fence that separates Shirley's backyard from the field, and (as far as I can tell) I'm just standing there, staring vacantly at nothing.

I close my eyes for a moment, take a breath, then open them again.

The fence isn't solid, it's the kind with upright posts joined together with horizontal timbers, so it's not blocking my view of the backyard or the back of the house, and although I've never seen either from this side of the fence before, there's no question that this is Shirley's house. There's not much light coming from it — the curtains are closed — and I don't seem to have the flashlight from the hillbilly's rifle anymore (I must have dropped it somewhere), but there's enough light coming from the houses to the right of Shirley's to let me see all I need to see. The ramshackle greenhouse, the little patio area in front of the window, the path that runs down the side of the house to a wrought-iron gate . . . I've seen them all before. And even if I didn't recognize them, I'd still know this was Shirley's house because it's the last one in the row — or the first one if you're coming into the village — and I can see from here that there isn't another house to the left of it.

I'm still feeling nothing but deadness as I hobble up to the fence — no relief that I'm finally here, no curiosity about what I might find, no joy at the prospect of seeing Mum again . . .

Nothing.

I'm not even scared anymore.

Just dead.

It's as if all the alarm circuits and fear mechanisms in my brain have been overloaded to such an extent that they've either crashed under the pressure, or they've automatically shut themselves down to avoid crashing under the pressure. I can still feel the big hole inside me where the fear should be, but it's empty now, just a hollow black chamber . . . a cave, a nothingness. The fear's gone, along with everything else I once had, and it's left me dead to the world.

Which is why, when a glint of light from Shirley's back window catches my eye, and I look over and see the edge of the curtain being pulled back, and a moment later the face of a nightmarish Santa Claus peers out . . .

I'm not scared.

I know I should be, because ever since that time in town when the monstrous Santa frightened me so much that I wet myself, I've been absolutely terrified of them.

But now . . . ?

I'm dead.

Everything's gone.

The moment I see the Santa looking out of Shirley's back window, I immediately move to my left and take cover behind a tree at the end of the fence. I stay there for a while, maybe thirty seconds or so, keeping myself out of sight as I try to figure out what the hell's going on, and then — having failed to come up with any kind of answer — I cautiously peer around the tree trunk at the house.

There's no one at the window now.

No nightmarish face.

The Santa's disappeared.

My first thought is that it was never there in the first place and that I'd just been seeing things again. I'm exhausted, freezing cold, out of my mind with pain . . . it's not surprising that my brain's playing tricks on me. And why on earth would there be a horror-Santa peering out of Shirley's back window anyway? It makes no sense at all.

But then I realize something.

The curtain isn't closed properly.

It looks as if it's caught on something. And I'm almost certain it wasn't like that when I first saw it. So someone must have pulled it back and peered out . . .

Someone.

It can't have been Shirley. She'd never leave the curtain like that. And it can't have been Mum either. She knows her sister's funny little ways so well that she'd never leave the curtain like that.

So it must have been someone else.

So maybe I didn't imagine the Santa after all.

There's only one way to find out, isn't there?

I check to make sure there's still no one at the window, then I step out from behind the tree and clamber over the fence into Shirley's backyard.

43

An Innocent Child

As I crouch down beneath the back window, in line with the gap in the curtain, and I slowly raise my head — inch by inch — until my eyes are just peeking over the sill, I'm momentarily convinced again that I really have lost my mind, and that I *am* seeing things that aren't there. What other explanation could there be for the vision I see through the glass?

Two Santa Clauses, both of them even nastier-looking than the monstrous nightmare of my childhood — two blood-red creatures, like hellish twins . . . two anti-Santas . . .

And one of them has a gun in his hand.

It's impossible.

It can't be real.

It has to be all in my mind . . .

But then I see Mum.

And I know, in an instant . . .

This is real.

She's sitting on the floor with Shirley, both of them bound and gagged, and they're both in a really bad state. Shirley's got an ugly gash on the side of her head, and Mum looks even worse. Her jaw's all swollen and discolored, and there's so much swelling and blackened bruising around her right eye that it's completely closed up. They're both deathly pale, and their ashen faces are stained with tears.

As I crouch there at the window, staring dumbstruck at Mum, a flood of feelings surges through me — rage, fear, love, hate, confusion, madness, violence, vengeance . . . all at once, all together, all uncontrollable and overwhelming.

Mum suddenly looks up at me then — it's as if she's felt my presence — and after a brief moment of stunned surprise, she glances anxiously at the anti-Santa with the gun, checking to make sure that he hasn't spotted me. When she sees that he's busy talking to the other anti-Santa on the other side of the room, she looks back at me — staring desperately into my eyes — and starts shaking her head.

The gesture's so vague it could mean anything, but I know what she's trying to tell me. She wants me to go, get away from here, don't get involved, it's too dangerous . . . please, just go . . . right now . . . before it's too late . . .

I sense rather than see the anti-Santa with the gun turning around, and I quickly duck down out of sight.

I don't know if he saw me or not, but it doesn't matter.

We'll be seeing each other in a few moments anyway.

There's nothing in my head as I cross over to the back door. No thoughts, no questions, no plans. And my heart is empty too. The flood of feelings has gone. I don't feel anything at all. I'm just doing what I have to do — whatever it takes, whatever needs to be done.

I'm not scared.

I'm dead.

Nothing in the world can frighten me.

The back door leads directly into the kitchen. The bottom half is solid wood, the top half is a glass panel. Shirley usually keeps it locked. I try the handle, just in case, but it doesn't open. I step back, raise the rifle, and crack the butt into the glass. It smashes loudly, the broken glass scattering all over the place, and there's no way the two Santas could have failed to hear it. I quickly reach in through the shattered glass — only vaguely aware of a sharp pain slicing into my gloveless hand — and then I turn the key in the lock, open the door, and step through into the kitchen.

It's a fairly small kitchen, a bit cramped, but clean and obsessively tidy. Halfway along the right-hand wall is an archway into a little dining room, and on the far side of the dining room a doorway leads through to the hallway, which in turn leads to the living room, the stairs, and the front door.

Just as I'm heading through the archway into the dining room, the anti-Santa-with-the-gun appears in the opposite doorway. We see each other at the same time, and as he stops in the doorway and levels his pistol at my head, I stop in the archway and raise the rifle to my shoulder, aiming it at his head.

The anti-Santa just stares at me for a moment — his eyes cold and hard, his jaw set tight — and then he blinks, and frowns, and looks me up and down, his brow furrowed, and then he shakes his head in disbelief, and his face breaks into a grin.

"Jesus Christ," he mutters, "what the hell are you?"

Gordon was still singing along to the radio as he approached the junction at the top of the village, and as he swung the Corsa to the right, without slowing down, the car skidded sideways across the road and the back end slammed into a drystone wall. The wall collapsed, and the Corsa's right rear wheel arch flew off, but Gordon just straightened the car, put his foot down, and sped off down the road toward the village.

"Suspect vehicle turned right onto Beckshill Lane, now heading south. He's coming your way, Griff."

"Do you want us to stop him?"

"Stay where you are for now. But be ready."

"Received."

Griff Beattie glanced at his partner. "Okay?"

Rick Tarn nodded, then reached down and started the car.

"Put the rifle down, kid," the anti-Santa-with-the-gun says dismissively. "You're not going to shoot me, are you?"

Without lowering the rifle, I take a step toward him. A flicker of doubt shows in his eyes — momentarily pricking his casual arrogance — and he instinctively steps back. He quickly regains his composure, straightening his gun arm and giving me a disdainful grin, but we both know it's too late for him. He stepped back. He can't change that now. He backed away from me.

"I don't want to hurt you, kid," he says, "but I will if I have to. So why don't you just put down the gun — "

"Get out of the way," I say, moving toward him.

My voice is calm and confident. It doesn't sound anything like me.

The anti-Santa is backing away again now, shuffling backward along the hallway, still aiming his gun at my head.

"All right, that's far enough," he says, trying to sound forceful. "I mean it. Any closer and I'll pull the trigger."

"No, you won't," I tell him. "I'm just a kid. You're not going to murder an innocent child, are you? You don't want to be locked up for the rest of your life."

He stumbles over his feet, regains his balance, then glances quickly over his shoulder to see where he's going. The stairs are on his right, the front door's behind him, and the living-room door is just to his left. It's half open. I can see the curtained front window — and in my mind, I can see Shirley's snow globe on the sill behind the curtains — and I can see the settee beneath the window, and some of the bookshelf beside it. But there's no sign of the second anti-Santa anywhere.

Not that I care.

I'm dead.

"But if I kill you," I say to the first anti-Santa, "if I shoot you dead, no one's going to blame me, are they? You broke into my auntie's house, you attacked her and my mum, you beat them up, tied them up, terrorized them . . . nothing's going to happen to me if I kill you. Nothing at all."

He's edging back into the living room now, nudging the door open with his elbow, and as I keep moving toward him, I begin to sense something — a distant voice, a faraway feeling, struggling to rise up through the deadness. It's too faint to make out clearly, but it feels — or sounds — like some kind of warning.

Everything happens in an instant then.

I see the first anti-Santa glance to his left, looking down at the far end of the room, where Mum and Shirley are tied to the radiator, and at the same time I hear the sound of muffled grunting and thumping coming from them. I react instinctively to it, and as I start moving toward the doorway, and the first anti-Santa starts getting out of my way, I see him flick a quick look behind me. It's an upward glance, and it's so rapid that it takes a moment to sink in, and by then it's too late. I spin around as fast as I can, but the second anti-Santa has already vaulted over the banister and is flying toward me, feetfirst.

A sudden (and totally useless) realization flashes through my mind — *Mum and Shirley did try to warn you, didn't they?* — and then a giant hammer slams into my head and everything goes black.

44

RIDING THE STARS

The roller-coaster world in Gordon's head had become his reality now. It was all there was to him, and all he wanted. To be up here in the endless black sky, riding the stars, the beautiful lights . . . a streak of silver flying high above the fields of white . . .

The Corsa was touching seventy miles per hour when it hit the first speed bump on the approach to the village. The car took off, all four wheels in the air, and the engine screamed . . .

"Whooohh!" cried Gordon.

Then, "Oomff!"

. . . as the Corsa crashed back down with a bone-jarring crunch. The trunk flapped open, a hubcap flew off — spinning across the road into a ditch — and as a loud metallic crack came from under the car, the front end dropped down and sparks started shooting out from the side.

To Gordon, the sparks were a mesmerizing blaze of burning stars, and he quickly realized that the faster he went, the brighter and fierier the stars became, so he put his foot down again, pushing the pedal all the way to the floor, and the screeching Corsa carried on speeding toward the village, leaving a trail of shooting stars in its wake.

"Charlie Three Zero, abandoning pursuit. Suspect vehicle is damaged, but still traveling at high speed. Safer to let him go. Three Four?"

"Go ahead," Beattie said.

"Don't try stopping him when he gets to you, okay? It's not worth the risk. Just let him go. We can pick him up later."

"Received."

Beattie clicked off his radio and looked at Tarn. "Did you hear what she said about stopping him?"

Tarn shook his head. "The radio went a bit crackly at that point, didn't it? I couldn't quite catch what she was saying. Could you make it out?"

"Nope, not a word of it."

Beattie smiled and fastened his seat belt.

Time is meaningless to me now — it doesn't seem to be passing anymore, it's just there, all of it, all at once . . . the past, the present, the future . . . it's all become the same thing . . . and I don't even know what that means — but I'm fairly sure that I'm only fully unconscious for seconds, not minutes, and I'm already semiconscious as the two anti-Santas drag me into the living room and drop me on the floor in front of Mum and Shirley. My head feels twice its normal size, and it's throbbing so violently that I can feel my brain thumping against my skull.

The pain isn't mine though. It belongs to another me. Not the other-me I was before, but a different me . . . a me that's everything and everywhere all at once — sprawled on the floor in front of Mum and Shirley . . . looking down at us from the ceiling . . . looking up through a snow-filled glass sky at a vast swathe of absolute blackness stretching deep into space for a thousand million miles . . .

And maybe we're all somewhere else too. Somewhere warm and soft and secure . . .

"I *told* you!"

The harsh voice brings me back to the me that's sprawled on the floor. It comes from behind me, and now I can hear the sound of a struggle — desperate movements, grunts, a muted yell . . . and then the harsh voice again —"Right, that's it!"— followed almost immediately by a muffled cry of pain . . .

It's Mum, I know it, and the sound of her suffering rips right through me, tearing all the chaos from my head, and in an instant, everything changes.

There's only me — there only ever was — and as I heave

myself up off the floor and start getting to my feet, there's only one thing that matters.

Everything is unnaturally clear to me now—the room, the anti-Santas, Mum and Shirley and me . . . I've never felt so focused in my life.

"Sit down, kid," I hear the first anti-Santa say.

He's across the room, his back to the front window, facing me. He's holding the pistol in both hands, arms outstretched, pointing the gun at me.

"Hey!" he barks, as I turn my back on him. *"Hey!"*

The second anti-Santa is standing over Mum and Shirley with the rifle in his hands. There's a fresh cut on the side of Mum's face, a small ring-shaped wound. It's bleeding, but not much, and it doesn't look too serious.

The first anti-Santa shouts at me again, but I take no notice. I've tuned him out for now. The second anti-Santa is wavering, not sure whether to point the rifle at me or keep it on Mum and Shirley. There's a small smear of red on the end of the rifle barrel, and I know how it got there. I can picture him getting annoyed with Mum—"I *told* you!"—and then, when she'd continued struggling—"Right, that's it!"—he'd jabbed her in the face with the rifle. I can tell from the look in his eyes that he didn't mean to hurt her, he was only trying to scare her, to make her shut up . . . he didn't mean it, honestly . . . he's not like that . . . he's sorry . . .

I go over to him, tear the rifle from his hands, and smash the butt into his head.

As he slumps heavily to the floor, I desperately want to look down at Mum. I want to tell her not to worry, don't be scared . . . I know what I'm doing . . . everything's going to be okay . . . but I know that if I look at her, even for a moment, this thing I've become will shatter into a million pieces and the fear will have me again, and then I'll just break down and die . . .

So I force myself to ignore Mum, and I turn around to face the other anti-Santa.

He's moved a few steps closer to me now, but he's still just standing there with his arms outstretched, pointing the gun at me. His hands are shaking, and there's a look of bewilderment in his eyes, but he's still got something in him — some kind of last-ditch pride — and we both know this isn't over just yet.

I drop the rifle and start moving toward him, walking slowly but steadily, my eyes fixed firmly on his.

He adjusts his feet, shuffling a bit, but this time he doesn't back off. He stays exactly where he is, staring down the barrel of the gun at me.

"You don't know what's going on here, do you?" he says. "I mean, you don't have a clue what any of this is about."

I don't say anything.

I take another step . . .

And another . . .

What is it, Elliot?

Nothing.

What did you see?

"It wasn't supposed to be like this," the anti-Santa says. His voice is distant and detached, as if he's talking to himself. "It should have been easy . . ."

Just tell me. What did you see?

It was snowing . . . like someone had shaken it up. That's what made me look at it. And I saw something . . . or I thought I did.

In the snow?

In the whole thing.

What was it?

". . . get in there, get him to open the safe, get the cash, and get out."

What was it, Elliot? What did you see?

I saw the deadness in my heart.

"Here he comes," Rick Tarn said. "You ready?"

Beattie nodded.

Tarn put the car into gear, tightened his seat belt, and edged out across the road. The two officers had already worked out the best place to block the road, so all Tarn had to do now was maneuver the patrol car into position. Once he'd done that, and they were both satisfied that nothing could get past them, Tarn turned off the engine, but left the lights on, and Beattie switched on the emergency lights.

I pause for a moment when the blue light starts flashing through the curtains. I'm only a few steps away from the anti-Santa now, and I can tell from the way he reacts to the lights that he's not surprised to see them.

"Police," he says simply. "They've been out there a while. I expect their backup just arrived." He smiles. "Now the fun's *really* going to start."

I'm beginning to lose myself now — or at least whatever self I've become — and I need to hold on to it, if only for a few more moments. So I wipe everything from my mind — the voices in my head, the strangely insistent memories, the pulsing blue light strobing around the room, making everything look weirdly stuttered — and I take another step toward the anti-Santa. This time he responds, stepping toward me and putting the barrel of the pistol to my forehead. I can feel it — cold and hard — pressing into my skin, and I can see his finger resting on the trigger.

"You're not right in the head, are you?" he says.

"Who is?"

He smiles again.

I know what he's doing, or at least planning on doing. I'm his way out of here, his hostage. The police won't risk anything if he's holding a gun to a kid's head.

But it doesn't matter.

It's not going to happen.

As I slowly raise my hand toward the pistol, I keep staring right into him, letting him see what's behind my eyes, letting him know what's there . . .

"Don't," he says. "No . . . don't be stupid . . ."

My hand rises to the gun, and I gently — but firmly — take hold of the barrel. I don't try to take the pistol off him, I just hold it.

"You can't kill me," I say, looking deep into his eyes. "I'm already dead."

45

FLESH AND BONE ON COLD STEEL

The patrol car was positioned sideways across the road, just a few yards down from Shirley's house. It was the narrowest part of the road—made even narrower by the cars parked on either side—and the blockade was so solid that even a cyclist would find it hard to get through.

With the emergency lights flashing, coloring the black sky with waves of blue, and the patrol car's headlights on full beam, the roadblock was unmissable, and Gordon saw it in plenty of time to stop.

Not that he had any intention of stopping.

Stopping meant a return to reality, and Gordon had had enough of that. He'd lived all his life in reality. He'd never known anything else. He'd never known he could be up here, riding the stars, riding the roller coaster, singing his heart out . . . and now that he did know, he was never going back.

It was as simple as that.

He was staying up here.

And nothing was going to stop him.

"What the hell's he *doing*?" Beattie said, staring in disbelief at the rapidly approaching car.

The front end of the Corsa on the driver's side was hanging down even more now. Sparks were still shooting out from under the car, half the front bumper was missing, and the left-side wheel arch had broken off and was jammed up under the chassis.

"He's not slowing down," Beattie said.

"He will."

"He'd better hurry up then. Unless he hits the brakes pretty soon, he's never going to stop in time."

The roadblock was less than thirty yards away now, and Gordon knew exactly what was going to happen when he got there. He could see it all in his mind, every little detail. It was as clear to him as if it had already happened. The shocked faces of the police officers as he hurtled toward them . . . the sudden fear in their eyes as they realized he wasn't going to stop . . . and then, at the moment of impact — or the moment of *expected* impact — their amazement and wonder as the Corsa became what it really was — a magnificent silver stallion — and instead of crashing into them, it took off into the air and, with one mighty bound, leaped effortlessly over the patrol car . . .

Gordon smiled.

That'll give them something to talk about.

There's nothing in the universe now but me and the anti-Santa. We're all there is, joined together by our eyes and the gun. My hand gripping the barrel, keeping it pressed to my head . . . his finger on the trigger, flesh and bone on cold steel . . . my eyes showing him my deadness, his showing me that there's a lot more to him than I thought. I can see his whole life in his eyes, and I can see the real possibility that this, for him, is where it's meant to end.

He doesn't fear it.

In fact, there's a part of him that welcomes it.

I feel an almost imperceptible movement in the pistol, and I don't have to look at it to know what it is. I can see it in his eyes — his finger is tightening on the trigger.

The tire blew just as the Corsa was passing the second house up from Shirley's. It was the front right tire, and the car was traveling at sixty-five miles per hour when it burst. As the Corsa veered violently to the right — angling in toward the line of parked cars — Gordon reacted instinctively, stamping on the brake pedal and yanking the steering wheel hard to the left.

The car turned just in time, narrowly missing a black Jeep parked in front of the Land Rover, but now the Corsa's wheels were locked up and it was skidding uncontrollably across the road in the opposite direction, still traveling at speed and heading straight for the houses . . .

Gordon was fighting the steering wheel, swinging it from side to side, desperately trying to control the skid, but he didn't really know what he was doing, and the car wasn't responding to anything he did anyway. It was as if it had a mind of its own, and it knew where it was going, and there was nothing anyone could do to stop it.

As it hurtled through a gap between two parked cars and mounted the sidewalk with a shuddering *thunk,* Gordon suddenly recognized what he was seeing through the windshield. The Volvo in the driveway to his right, the low picket fence straight ahead, and on the other side of the fence the snow-covered patch of lawn—which he dutifully mowed every Sunday in the summer—and beyond that the all-too-familiar house that had been his home since the day he was born . . .

Gordon smiled.

"It's fate," he muttered.

As the Corsa smashed through the picket fence and careened across the snow-whitened lawn toward the house, Gordon took his foot off the brake and let go of the steering wheel.

*

We both hear it at the same time, and without changing position or letting go of the gun, we both instinctively look over at the front window. The sound we hear is familiar, but wrong. It's obviously a car, but it's not the kind of sound a car usually makes when it's passing by, and it's rapidly getting louder and closer ... *much* closer ... and all we seem able to do is stand there in the middle of the room, frozen together in our absurd pose, both of us staring numbly at the curtained front window.

We hear a shuddering *chunk,* then a loud crash of splintering wood ... then a fleeting moment of relative silence ... and then, with a thunderous crash, the room explodes.

46

THE FEAR

It's all over in a matter of seconds — the massive crash as the car demolishes the living-room wall, the violent eruption of bricks and metal and broken glass flying across the room . . . the air choked with dust and smoke . . . the hazy awareness that something terrible is happening . . . then a sudden shattering pain in my head . . .

Then nothing.

Nothing . . .

Less than nothing. An unimaginable emptiness, a vast swathe of absolute blackness stretching deep into space for a thousand million miles . . .

And then it starts all over again.

The massive crash as the car demolishes the living-room wall, the violent eruption of bricks and metal and broken glass . . .

Then it stutters . . .

Stops.

Starts again.

The massive crash as the car demolishes the living-room wall . . . the floor tilting as the room is turned upside down

shake it

like this

and then a blizzard suddenly explodes out of nowhere, a great white whirlwind of bricks and metal and broken glass swirling and tumbling all around me . . . and now I can see the big bad wolf. He's standing right in front of me, dressed in a Santa costume and wearing a long white beard, and as I gaze into his curiously human eyes, I see a familiar face reflected in their mirrored darkness — a haunted face, battered and bruised, covered in scratches, caked in dirt and dry blood — and I think I know who it is . . . I'm *sure* I know who it is . . . but just as it's coming to me, on the tip of my tongue, a spinning brick comes flying out of nowhere and hits the wolf in the head, and as he falls to the ground everything melts away . . .

The blizzard, the wolf, the haunted face . . .

All gone.

Never was.

And then there's nothing again.

Nothing . . .

Less than nothing. An unimaginable emptiness . . .

Elliot?

A voice from the other side of the universe.

Can you hear me?

And then it starts all over again.

The massive crash as the car demolishes the living-room wall . . .

It's different now. It's the same — the same crash, the same car, the same wall — but it all feels more distant, more fragile, as if it's real but not real . . . and I'm there, but I'm also somewhere else . . . somewhere halfway between . . . somewhere soft and white . . . and the violent eruption of bricks and metal and broken glass is silent and slow and somehow graceful

Elliot?

Can you hear me?

and something is going *beep beep beep* and another voice says

It's all right, nothing to worry about.

and then everything goes quiet again and I'm back in Shirley's living room and all I can see — in silent slow-motion — is the snow globe flying out from the heart of the eruption and shooting across the room toward me.

The snow globe . . .

Everything.

There's nothing else now. The rest of the world has gone — the room, the car, the bricks and metal and glass, the dust and smoke . . . it's all disappeared into an unseen darkness, and all that's left is the snow globe and me. It shines with a soft and silvery luminescence, and as it tumbles and spins through the void toward me, I can already feel the shattering pain as it hits me in the head . . . I can physically *feel* it . . . it's there, right there . . . right between my eyes . . .

I raise my hand to my head, feeling for the pain . . . but my arm gets stuck, caught up in something. I yank it, and as my arm comes free, I feel a sharp pain in my wrist . . . and when I put my hand to my head, it doesn't feel right

You're not right in the head, are you?

it doesn't feel like skin, it feels like some kind of cloth. I try to get hold of it

No, Elliot . . .

but something takes hold of my hand and gently pulls it away

Is he awake?

and now the snow globe is right in front of me, within touching distance, and as it moves closer and closer I can see it's not tumbling and spinning anymore, it's still . . . perfectly still . . . I can see it with absolute clarity. It's right in front of my eyes now. I can see the wolf, and the pathway through the woods, and the falling snow . . . and I can see the red-hooded figure of the little girl with the basket

Ellamay?

and she turns her head and looks out through the glass at me

Elliot?

Please come back . . .

and now the little girl's face is right in front of me, staring into my eyes . . . and for a moment her face is mine — battered and bruised, covered in scratches, caked in dirt and dry blood — and then it's ours, together, Ellamay's and mine

We are as one

and then it changes again and it's Mum's. She looks terrible — her face covered in stitched-up cuts, her right eye blackened and swollen shut

Elliot?

Can you hear me?

her skin deathly white . . .

I think he might be waking up.

She doesn't look anything like herself.

Wake up, Elliot

it's me . . .

The snow globe shatters.

My glass skull cracks.

"Please, Elliot . . . please wake up . . ."

My eyes flutter open.

I'm in a white room, lying on a white bed, staring up at a white ceiling. My head hurts. I can feel things sticking into my skin, something gripping my hand. My mouth is bone-dry. Muted sounds are drifting all around me — soft beeps, a low humming, hushed voices in the background — and just for a moment I'm a newborn baby again, lying on my back in an incubator, looking up through the clear-plastic dome at the white sky of the ceiling above . . . and suddenly the sky darkens and an unknown thing appears out of nowhere, and as it looms down over me, getting bigger and bigger all the time, the fear erupts inside me — uncontrollable, overwhelming, absolute . . .

I close my eyes.

I can feel it . . .

The fear.

I can feel it then, and I can feel it now.

But it feels different now . . .

It somehow feels right.

It's still wrong — how can it ever be right to be so afraid? — but it's *my* wrong. It's me. It's how I'm supposed to be.

Not dead.

I'm not dead anymore.

I'm scared.

I'm me again.

I open my eyes.

"Oh, thank God," I hear Mum say.

I turn to the sound of her voice and see her sitting next to me on the edge of the bed. She's holding my hand, gripping it tightly. Tears are pooling in her eyes.

She smiles at me.

"Welcome back, Elliot," she says.

I smile at her.

Yeah, echoes Ellamay. *Welcome back, Elliot. Happy Christmas.*

And I smile at her too.